Saturn Returns:
The Private Papers of
A Reluctant Astrologer

Elizabeth Spring

ISBN: 1-4610-9361-9
ISBN-13: 9781461093619

Dedication

With Love to~
Harry, Sarah, Shane, Tallulah & Greta
And for all Readers
Who love the language of astrology~
The romance of sacred places
and the pursuit of mysteries
of all kinds~

Table of Contents:

Part One

Part Two: Isabelle's Book: Saturn Returns

Prologue

"Sometimes we transit each other like benevolent planets."

To: Kendra@gmail.com
Subject: Our email letters

Dear Kendra~

Thank you for your kind letter—and the answer is yes! I'd love to write and mentor you in astrology and to share with you how I'm navigating through this Saturn Return! I'm touched by the coincidence, the synchronicity, of your letter coming to me at this time—you, at the age of twenty-nine in your first Saturn Return, and me at the age of fifty-nine in my Second Saturn Return. I don't know why we are coming into each other's lives now, but I sense a sweet synchronicity here—a meeting of minds and hearts, perhaps.

I think your idea of "email correspondence" is great, as I've always loved the idea of letters. People don't write that way anymore, but our emails—our letters—would be our "private papers" between us.

I'm going to be really honest with you in these email letters. Kendra, I don't want to keep up a "wise woman persona" with you—the mask of the professional astrologer—and so

I'd like to ask you if you'd keep these letters just between us, until...well, I don't know. At least for now. Professionalism creates false barriers at times, and I think it's a little dishonest, even a little lonely......but I do want to share with you my writings on Saturn and why I see myself as the "the reluctant astrologer."

Sophie said you could be trusted and she thought we were kindred spirits. She says you are very curious and love to read~is that true? In these emailings and journal entries you'll see how astrology entwines with life in strange ways—what an interesting way to learn astrology—but no charts in the beginning—too many details will confuse.

And...you'll see that my life is far from perfect. I may know more about some things than others do, but you'll see that despite my "astrological foresight" my family has been pulled apart by philosophical differences. Maybe what has torn us apart can bring us back together. You see, it's not all written yet....

In your first email, you said that other astrologer—the famous one—filled you with fear. It sounded like he intimidated you by saying that your Saturn Return is going to be a "rough ride" filled with undertows and swells beyond your control—who would want an astrologer like that? If anything, I see myself as a psychic cheerleader and counselor, not as a fortune teller who foretells bad times approaching.

But—I must agree that Saturn Returns are testy times, and yet the rewards of getting through them with integrity are great. Saturn Returns are times that call us to find our courage and to release our fears. It's as if we are now being called to create something new we can depend on. I believe if we're willing to make the necessary changes the reward is great. That's what Saturn wants—to build or rebuild a part of our lives. Do you know what that is for you?

There is something you should know about me—I used to believe in "predictions." Now I know "it's complicated." (Yes, I know that's the phrase people use on-line in dating or facebook sites—instead of single or married.) That's the way I feel about astrology at times…it's complicated and I'm a bit reluctant. Was I fated to be an astrologer? Am I fated to be in a complicated marriage? I question it all.

Sometimes I wonder if I'm repeating an old karmic pattern or if this soul-work connects the threads of my life, making patterns and a richer tapestry. I think so. I love thinking how we each are part of a larger whole and how deeply connected we all are to each other. But sometimes I forget.

So yes, it's complicated—and that's why I see myself as a reluctant astrologer. I have a radical belief in free will and that our choices make all the difference.

That said, it was simply wrong for that astrologer to fill you with fear. I guess he would say, like the ancient astrologers once said, that "Saturn has returned" and now we are up against our fate! Hah! Don't believe the doomsayers.

But Saturn was once feared, and seen as an old man.... but that old man could be seen as a wise old man, like my teacher-mentor, Carl Jung. I wish I had known him—do you remember him? He was a Swiss psychologist who was once a colleague of Sigmund Freud. Of course he's not alive and he never "mentored" me, but I feel as if he is with me always. I have his photograph on the wall in my study, and under it one of his famous sayings: "When a given situation is not made conscious, it happens outside as fate." That's always given me something to think about, though I wonder if I have the wisdom to understand it.

That's the question, isn't it? How much can we change by our choices, and how much is fated. Jung's whole life was about bringing what is unconscious into consciousness. I really believe that the effort to do that will make all the difference for us at these Saturn Returns. And I'd dare say your life is not going to go the way any astrologer would predict for you—you are coming into your true Self now.

So we will write. Let's see how it goes...sometimes I think friends can 'transit' each other like benevolent planets.

Fondly,

~ Isabelle

To: Kendra@gmail.com
Subject: *Sorry, I forgot to say that…*

…the most radical thing I can say about astrology is that I believe it has nothing to do with the planets and stars! I believe it works for mysterious reasons that are not based on any "woo-woo vibrations" of the planets upon our psyches. If I had to say why it works, I might point to Carl Jung's theory of synchronicity to try to explain. Do you know about that?

Synchronicity simply means "meaningful co-incidence." It speaks of an unexplainable connection between an outer physical event and an inner 'emotional' event that is not normally related—such as when a clock stops working at the hour of a person's death. Or when you "accidently" meet someone you haven't seen in ten years just at a moment you were thinking about them. Synchronicity happens, I believe, because it's a moment of meaningfulness if we can understand it. The universe, like astrology, is not random or purposeless, but it is "an art" to be able to decipher "the meanings" that surround us.

I deeply believe in this language of the Soul, but I sense that a little knowledge of astrology can be a dangerous thing. It can feed our fears and vulnerabilities rather than our hopes. I try not to fall into that trap when I see 'hard transits' coming, but sometimes I do look at my chart and sigh. I do fear at times—you'll see. But then I remind myself of all the possible ways, both good and not so good, that planets and signs can play themselves out.

So you will see that I don't think the same way many predictive astrologers do. I forget how much astrology you know. It doesn't really matter. Astrological prediction is more like a finger pointing to the Moon, and saying "Ah…look!" I think we have been given this particular map of the psyche, this directional compass, as a way of knowing some things—but it still points to a Mystery that will not fall on its knees before the chart of any scientist or astrologer.

So dear Kendra, I give you this story, my story, which is simply the story of one astrologer. I hope that when you finish reading it you will have a better understanding not only of astrology but those things that can tear love apart and pull love back together again. It all intertwines, doesn't it?

Hmm…I just remembered something the Christian monk, Thomas Merton, once said: "Before we can become who we really are, we must become conscious of the fact that the person who we think we are, may be an imposter and a stranger." Something to ponder? I think it relates to Saturn.

Enough for now~till later then!

Fondly,

~Isabelle

Chapter 1
Newport to Boston, 2011

"It is never too late to be who you might have been."
George Eliot

"The prediction's coming true..." I moaned aloud to no one, clutching tight to the steering wheel as the winds buffeted the car about as it crested the top of the Newport Bridge. Talking to myself would be a good way to keep awake. I was exhausted from the effort of leaving Peter and home—from the effort of keeping back my fear of this Saturn Return.

"I don't believe in predictions, and I am choosing to leave." I grumbled. How could I keep my mind on my driving? I thought how everything felt worse because I was the predictor—the astrologer. I couldn't blame anyone else, but couldn't this be seen differently? Predictions meant something had to happen, and one could only react. This was different, wasn't it?

What comforting words would an astrologer tell a client? What could I tell myself about how such a transit of these planets might play out in my life? I knew only too well the dangers of the Saturn Return when the "ancient malefic" Saturn was constricting and conjuncting my Sun, Saturn and Venus in the 7th house of marriage. And I knew only too well how the upcoming transit of Pluto, the Lord of the Underworld, would also be "squaring off" to my Sun and challenging me for this next year. Both Saturn and Pluto were demanding change, and so I was changing—determined to co-operate with these *archetypal gods* rather than let them overthrow me. I was not going to be predictable if I could help it, but what was the change that was needed?

I hate astrological words like *malefics* and *benefics.* Those heavily laden words were used in the ancient astrological texts and have a way of lingering in the psyche. I reminded myself how life is less fated than it used to be—we have so much more choice—but I was scared. I wasn't going to just sit there and let those *malefics* roll over me. I wasn't dead yet. I wasn't even divorced... not yet.

If I had been doing a "reading" for someone I would have found a way to discuss making bridges rather than "flying over" them like I was doing now on this bridge. I would tell them not to look down or to look back, as they crossed over bridges both metaphorical and real. I would reassure them that they could handle any storm and not be afraid. But instead now, I looked down beneath me and shivered. The waters below were whipping themselves into menacing omens of white capped fury.

Was it foolish to think I could outrun the furies? Accelerating—a pulsing wave of adrenaline surged through me—or maybe that was a hot flash? Another gust of wind shook the car. I looked down and out to the wild ocean below me once more and decided that was enough looking and pondering. No more looking back, no more astrological metaphors, please.

I took the right turn exit onto Rt 95. Better to be on land during a storm, yet the curve felt slippery and my neck tightened. The windshield was fogged; the sleet had turned to icy snow and swirled in front of my eyes. Oh yes, any speed more than 40 MPH could turn into a slide and spin. I had to hold tight and focus. I was going to reach Boston by dusk, and check into that little hotel downtown—the one that I had walked by and admired many times.

I laughed out loud, but the brain chatter continued: Was it cynical now, thinking about the word: "transformative"? I was sick of all the euphemisms astrologers used to describe life and death situations—real or metaphorical. How do you describe the terrain of death, rebirth and hard choices? How do you describe the irritants of change? *Like a grain of sand in an oyster*, of course, that's what I used to say. *We need to secrete our "wise juices" around these irritants to create the pearl of wisdom.* If my old life was dying, I needed to find a way to preserve the pearl inside me.

I remembered what had started this. I was reading the poets Rumi and Hazrat Khan…such dangerous lovers of men and God! And I came across this: *"I looked for Thee on the earth: I searched for Thee in the heavens, my Beloved, but at last I have found Thee hidden as a pearl in the shell of my heart."* Dangerous words to someone seeking their Soul. Where's the pearl of Wisdom in my heart? Life isn't as simple and deep as I wished it was. I could do better. And then there was that day I found these words from Oscar Wilde: *"Falling in love with yourself is the beginning of a life-long romance."*

Oh, I had drifted far from that! But maybe, like the phoenix, I'm rising from the ashes now. That feels good—I'm that "metaphorical bird" that was burnt in the flames, and now was rising again out of my own ashes. I don't know if it felt more like being a re-born phoenix or an oyster in need of creating a pearl? Maybe I'm just a woman running away from a life she has outgrown.

I needed to stop thinking and focus. My hands gripped the steering wheel as if the car was going to go out of control at any minute. The windshield wipers fought fast against the mesmerizing swirls of oncoming snow. I hate this. I turned the music up high. Maybe it could turn fear into excitement or maybe it could help me calm down. Ah—the Eagles were singing "Desperado"....oh yes, "you've got to let somebody love you before it's too late." Too late? That was depressing.

I switched the channel—Andrea Boccelli singing "Time to Say Goodby." Oh yes, that was better...old songs, so uncannily accurate in their timing, in their synchronistic message. I was leaving Peter after twenty years of marriage. I didn't feel loved anymore; not the way I wanted to feel love. That was the short version.

I snapped the music off. There would be no more tears; I'm going on an adventure. "Auspicious or un-auspicious"—this transit was not going to be a prediction of misery. Peter was right though—I held too much fear, I had fallen under the impact of panic attacks before, but now I'm giving myself "wings" and….. I'm the pearl in the making; right? I'm going to find the Self that I could fall in love with again.

The cars ahead of me were slowing down as they rounded another corner—but there, streaking across the sky was another striking line—a blush of pink—-looking like an arrow leading me on. Here was a good sign: here was Venusian beauty, a comforting touch. That would have to be enough for the moment.

Maybe another hour at most, and then I'd be on my old stomping grounds on Beacon Hill again. Reaching into my bag with one hand I tried to retrieve my cell phone. Who could I talk to now? No one.

~

There were no stars tonight…no ancient guidance, but instead a slippery road. My fear was escalating into incessant chatter with my "inner astrologer." What could I say to ease the possible malefic effects of Saturn? I heard myself mimicking my counseling voice: "And what do you think about vitamin supplements during this time, or anti-depressants? Do you have a support system or someone you can count on now?" My interior monologue wouldn't stop, and I could hear that smile in my voice when I would ask a client: "Have you looked at your North Node? It's like the North Star—you can use it to find your way." There were no stars tonight.

The prediction of death and endings had become easier to speak of metaphorically, and the rebirth following the deaths, but sometimes it simply isn't a metaphor. Sometimes it's a slippery road at dusk. Sometimes you die.

The storm was easing up.... I could see the fading light of the December afternoon was beautiful as I approached Providence. The highway lights had starkly outlined the bare tree branches making them look like upraised arms—like the arms of people yearning for something. I like to search for the words to an image—what was it those trees looked like? People—they looked like people raising their arms to God, yearning for love. Those trees had deep roots, something I didn't have now.

And what about this moment—this gritty cold reality? I held on, knowing it would pass like everything else—but as soon as I could see the lights of Boston, the cars ahead were slowing down. It was looking like a major traffic jam. It was a bad transit. In the past I'd always thought of *a transit* as simply being what was happening in the sky at the moment. I would look at a client's transits to know what planets were aspecting their birth chart. I'd make a bi-wheel on my computer and be able to read the future...just a little. In this case I'd be thinking: Saturn, the planet of limitation, frustration, and melancholy was transiting—dancing—with Venus, the goddess of love. No, I wouldn't say that, yet I would bet they weren't having a good time. What a cheerful dancer Saturn could be! Hah...like a grumpy old man.

But maybe the unpredictable and rebellious planet Uranus would throw in something I never expected—and maybe Uranus, that oddball planet could give Saturn a little help in guiding me through Pluto's underworld, as Pluto squares off to my Sun.

Of course that was a "worse-case scenario-prediction" and few people have the line-up of those planets arranged on their chart the way I did—all those challenging squares, conjunctions and oppositions as part of their Saturn Return. I'm determined to make the best of it. "No transit happens before its time" I would always say. Astrology had a sacred geometry to it that I trusted—and within it, was freedom. It all depends how we chose to play the aspects out.

As an astrologer, I would always say to others that challenging transits could be played out well with a dose of patience and insight. But now, what was this jammed up transit of mine? So what if Saturn was making his "Return" and Pluto was squaring off to him as well? I was going to play it out with all the courage I could summon, and in this case, it meant leaving my marriage to Peter and starting out again. I needed a new beginning.

I sighed at the long slow lineup of cars approaching the city. I'd get there, but this was tiring; an accident on the side of the road had slowed everything down and looked foreboding. A car had flipped over. I passed the squashed car slowly and hoped there had not been a death.

As we inched along, I could feel myself beginning to space out....oh, the perpetual litany of my astrological talk was tiresome at times. The car in front of me stopped short, as I slammed on the brakes and swerved from hitting it.

Wake up! I scolded myself. "Pay attention to the divine timing of things" I used to say. *Pay attention* was going to be my *mantra* now. I was going to do something different, and I was going to pay attention; to be as conscious as I could. Yet I was divinely impatient. The lineup of cars had come to a complete stop. I sat for at least 10 minutes without moving. Then I reached over to my new leather journal and re-read this morning's entry:

December 9th 2011

I can't believe I'll be leaving Peter this afternoon—after over twenty years of marriage. But I'm packed and ready. Boston will be good—I will just leave with no threats of divorce, harsh words, or messiness. I told Peter last night that it was simply a chance for me to refind myself. Did he even know I was lost? There were no bitter accusations...but what are my choices now? Here I am, a woman with a Libra Sun—

the most indecisive of all the signs—daring to be decisive. Can I do this?

I looked up and saw the traffic beginning to move. Closing the journal I whispered to myself: "God I need you, now...please, help me." And then the cars began to move on. As I tucked the journal back into my bag, I let my hands caress the smooth leather cover. I loved its burgundy color with its Celtic "triple swirl mandala" imprinted on the cover: the numinous threes: maiden, mother, crone. Past, present, future. Body, mind, spirit. The trinity of God and the trinity of the family. What would prove to be true and lasting? I only knew that my journal would be my constant companion now.

Chapter 2

"And then the knowledge comes to me that I have space within me for a second, timeless larger life." Rilke

It took longer to get to Beacon Hill than I hoped. I circled round the hotel looking for a parking spot till I remembered that I could park underneath the Boston Commons. I descended into the parking lot, circled around again, and got out, heaving my one large bag over my shoulder. My glazed eyes met other glazed eyes as I walked through the garage and across the park. I wished I felt safe, I wished the familiarity of the place held me more, but all I could do was shiver. I was simply a single woman walking alone, at night, in a city.

I couldn't tell at first glance if the hotel was quaint or a bit seedy. Too late for that now, I thought, so I put on my "matter-of-fact professional persona" and checked in. It might as well have been a mental hospital because "I" was barely there. Dissociated, is what they might call it. The clerk yelled loudly to a bored looking young porter: "Isabelle Cocroft, Room 311" He startled me. "Isabelle Cocroft, Room 311" he repeated louder, awakening me and the porter.

So this is who I am now: a middle aged woman staying for an indefinite period of time at a questionable hotel. The porter threw my bag on his shoulder and showed me to the room. I gave him a couple of dollars and hoped for a smile in return, but he pulled out his cell phone before even closing the door.

I looked at the room and looked down at my feet. I felt a little dizzy. Who was this Isabelle now—the one standing alone in this room? The one who felt like she was losing her mind? Certainly Peter Cocroft would be thinking she'd be staying for one night only, and would be returning to Rhode Island and resuming her normal life tomorrow. But there was no Peter Cocroft here, only this "Isabelle Cocroft of Room 311" who was checking in for a week, because she just didn't know what else to do.

What was happening? Where was Isabelle the mother of Sophie, and the loyal Mrs. Isabelle Cocroft? Who was this 'good mother' now that her only child was barely out of college? I sighed and gritted my teeth. A little anger can be good fuel for action, I thought, but who is this person who is now authoring this chapter of my life? Was I still the same person as the twenty-four year old Isabelle who once knew all the back streets of Beacon Hill, and loved strolling through Boston's Public Garden? Where was the Isabelle who used to wear her blond hair in a loose bun on top of her head, and who had once had a thriving astrology business right here, right on Charles Street?

I snapped out of my reverie and looked cursorily at the expensive tiny room. Black, white, chrome, modern; totally not me. Minimal décor and maximum function. I turned around and walked out. I wasn't going to sit there alone. It had been two years ago that I had walked by this tiny hotel and wondered what it would be like to stay here. Now I knew.

I closed the door with a snap, hurried down the stairs and flew out into the street. The little white lights of the Christmas season were twinkling on the trees and shops, and the snow had stopped. The trees were drooping down languorously under the weight of the winter snow, and the benches in the Public Garden looked like they were buried under memories long gone.

I didn't pause to look at anyone or anything till I could see the hill and the busy corner of Charles and Beacon Street. Beacon Hill is a city within a city. The oldest part of Boston, its brick and brownstone buildings cluster together on a hill beside the Charles River. Its narrow streets and well-tended doorways and window-boxes give it a cared for look, and one could argue that its gentrification was a bad thing or a good thing, but the hill itself maintains its own character; a kind of stony tenaciousness that never changes too much.

The locals as well as the visitors merge seamlessly along its narrow streets and alleyways, and the hill is home to both students and working people. The Public Garden is its pearl, with its magnolia trees and rose gardens in the spring, and its old fashioned street lamps and skating pond in winter. I love how the streets around it are named after moods, like "Joy Street" or nature: "Acorn Street" or historical figures, like "Revere Street". I love how the old swampland along the river was rebuilt...the streets now gently slope down to the river in an area known as "the flats." I couldn't help but think that if Charles Dickens were alive today he would undoubtedly be living in one of the old brownstones with a shiny black door with a polished knocker. Here is where my past and future were meeting again, and here was where my grandmother lived in 1904.

Charles Street cuts a gentle curve through the hill, and the busy street was full of shops and small eateries. I walked up one side of Charles St and down the other trying to find a quiet restaurant, and decided on a small pizza place that served wine. I would sit there till my mood changed. The wine surely would help with my "attitude adjustment."

But it didn't happen quite like that. I sat and ate, and drank two glasses of wine while staring out the window at the people walking their dogs and hurrying home from work. I was debating whether I dare order a third glass, when I saw there was a line of people waiting for a table. I knew that the right thing to do was to move on. And so I did, back to the hotel and the surly porter. He looked up at me quickly, then returned again without a word to his computer game. I was shocked by my invisibility.

The next morning I ordered a bagel sandwich and coffee at the corner coffee shop. Then I do what I always do: I opened my laptop and brought up the astrological aspects for the day. The moon was in Cancer, ruling over the three H's of "home, heart, and hearth" and was in a harmonious aspect, a "trine" to Jupiter. Jupiter, the planet of luck and opportunity—an "ancient benefic" in the old astrological texts—was a marker for where we are sometimes 'graced' with opportunities. The Moon was all about emotion. Even this fleeting trine aspect between the Moon and Jupiter could be good. It was surely not one to waste. And with the Sun in optimistic Sagittarius, I was going to seize the moment. The work I had before me was clear. I needed to find a place to live—a Saturnian task.

I was responsible, wasn't I? I had 'saturnized' my relationship with Peter; seeing him in a negative light, and now it remained to be seen how we would play it out. Did he abandon me first or was I abandoning him? It seemed like he had been drifting away from me first, and I had just now become aware of it. But the Moon looked good today, even if it only held hints of possibilities, and Saturn was calling me to action. Abandonment and guilt issues would have to wait.

Having the Moon in good aspect to grace-filled Jupiter was as motivating as the caffeine. With a last bite of bagel and the last sip of coffee I bolted for the door.

It felt good to join the mass of humanity again bustling on the street. It was hard to be lonely with all this busyness around. I walked past the fancy pizza place I had gone to last night and finally came to a window filled with listings of apartments for rent on the hill. The prices were high, but perhaps I could rent a simple studio; no frills. Still the commitment of a year's lease was daunting. I would have to sign on the dotted line. But Mercury was retrograde—not a good time to make a decision or to sign on the "dotted line."

And...maybe if I walked around a little more I could rally enough courage to go inside a real estate office and sit down with a real person, state my case, and tell my story. Yes, that was the idea. But first I needed to gain courage—-I would walk around the block first. But I had worn the wrong shoes. They were too delicate and my feet kept slipping on the ice or stumbling in between the cracks in the brick sidewalks. Everywhere I looked there were sensible people hurrying off to work—half of them talking on cell phones—and all the morning people walking their dogs. A few of them looked me in the eye as they passed and smiled.

Back when I had lived here in my twenties, the hill wasn't quite such a "well-heeled place" and I didn't know if I could really afford to move here now. But memories of love and music were all centered here, and that was what had pulled me back. Neptune: music, no boundaries, illusions and love; Requited or unrequited, it didn't matter. Neptune's addictions and pleasures were sticky.

I was nearing the street with the old Swiss-German house when I decided to detour down a side street towards the flats. "Better slow down" I kept reminding myself, as I nearly fell again on the ice. Giving my feet a rest I leaned up against a wall. What? It looked like there was a "For Rent" sign up in the tiny paned window of my old shop—could it be?

Hobbling over, I peered inside the small room where my astrology shop used to be in those years when I first met Peter. Could this really be up for rent? I felt a shiver run through me. This kind of synchronicity-coincidence doesn't happen in real life.

I looked into the small dark room and could see how the walls were chipped and peeling paint was everywhere. I could see the faded outline where old pictures used to be—so many years of tenants coming and going had left their mark, but still it had that old world charm—but where was the fireplace? It looked like someone had boarded it over, and it looked like there was more room in the back but I couldn't see.

I remembered the goddess face in the fireplace...I had loved her closed eyes and serene expression. How could someone have covered over that beautiful fireplace? Now she wasn't there to tell me what had happened there in all those years since I had left. But maybe she was still there, underneath all that veneer. And was that a staircase in the back—was it leading to other rooms above?

How expensive could this be? Could I afford it? But this was just a space to work in, how could I pay for an apartment as well? I couldn't. A Libra with a dilemma. Libra is ruled by Venus, and this was a very attractive Venusian space—but—but what was the choice here? Not really any, except for desire…I desired that room. That was what I wanted. No ambivalence; what a welcome feeling.

Taking down the phone number on the *For Rent* sign, I walked back to a cappuccino shop on the opposite corner and ordered one of those oversized cups full of coffee and chocolate. The young waiter there looked Italian, with thick dark hair swept back. He had a large intricate Celtic tattoo on his arm and he let his arms gesture freely as he talked. He was working with pleasure…and he kept returning to ask me if he could get me anything else. What a sweet guy, I thought.

I could see him watching me as I took out my cell phone and called the realtor's number I had written on the scrap of paper. I was expecting an answering machine. I froze. "Yes, of course, of course, I can be there in thirty minutes" I said.

And so I waited. The waiter seemed to be watching me. If I had been younger, or if I lived here, I would know this man, this waiter. We would be friends, we would know some of the same people and he would tell me stories about his girlfriend or boyfriend. Maybe he would be a client.

But it wasn't then, it was now; the waiter returned with the check. I noticed he signed it "Thank you, Carlos" with a swirl. Maybe he was a calligrapher as well as a waiter. I looked over at him and saw him smiling at me. I left a couple of dollars, and as I made my way towards the door I simply exchanged a few words about the weather and the coffee. But I let myself look into his eyes just a second too long, and he, who was not unfamiliar with this happening, simply touched my shoulder lightly with his hand, and wished me a good day. I had been seen by someone.

Finally feeling visible, I floated towards the door. I paused for a second, and instead of opening it I saw a small bulletin board behind it. The board was covered with messages and notices, and I allowed myself to linger there, looking at nothing and everything. Then I reached into my bag, took out a small pen and note paper, and scribbled on it: "It is never too late to be who you might have been. George Eliot." Taking a tack, I attached it to the board and grinned. I was sure now in my intention.

❧

Could I really do this? Could I do something so quickly? Could I dare spend money so quickly—on me, on this, now? I knew it had to be somewhat out of my price range, but then again I wasn't sure what that really was.

The realtor had the key to the office on a peg board behind him and in no time he was unlocking the black door and turning the old latch. The room still smelled like fireplace ashes, though there was no fireplace to be seen. I pointed to where the wall was pushed out and where the fireplace had once been.

"There used to be a black marble fireplace here" I said to the realtor, "with the imprint of a Goddess face in the metal insert…it was stunning." He looked surprised I would know this.

"I could ask the landlord if this could be uncovered, if you agreed not to make fires here." His hand knocked against the cheap paneled wood covering.

"Yes…..and what's that?" I asked pointing to a spiral metal staircase that looked like it led up to something.

"There's a studio apartment upstairs…come see."

I followed the realtor up the steep curling staircase to the second floor. I kept telling myself to calm down, that it was going to be too expensive and that it needed too much work. But there it was—one good sized room with a kitchen and a bath, and a bay window that overlooked the street below. I loved it! I loved everything about it—even the peaked slant of the ceiling and how it made the sunlight into patterns across the walls. It was a classic garret with a skylight and a tiny slanted alcove that I could turn into a writing nook. It needed work, but I was more than willing.

I asked the price, and computed the price of two in one—apartment and office. "Yes," I said immediately. "Yes." I said, feeling the guilt of renting this space was so delicious—I was afraid to show my excitement. I could feel my face twitch. "Can you get the fireplace opened?"

"I'm sure I can. I know the owner." The realtor grinned as if he knew my secrets, my past. I can barely remember walking back with him to his office; he made a couple of phone calls, our heads were nodding. I was staring out the window at an orange cat walking confidently along on the brick pavement outside; he looked like he knew where he was going—he looked like my cat. And I was signing papers...the lease, the check....how could it all happen so fast?

Walking back to the hotel, I remember stopping off again and peeking in the window at the space where my new life would be. It would need some work—I could do the cleaning and painting. Then I treated myself to lunch with wine, at the same Italian restaurant, and felt like I'd been transported into a romantic fantasy. I let the feeling linger...

That night I called Sophie from the hotel. Peter had already told her about my leaving and I could hear the pain and coolness in her voice. She had a hard time understanding why I had left, and I wished I had called sooner or at least before Peter had told her his version of our story.

Sophie didn't seem to get it. I kept telling her how much I still loved Peter but that I had to leave. There were long pauses. I asked her about a boyfriend whom she had met at some new church group, but she was reluctant to talk about anything.

"Why couldn't you have stayed in Newport instead of moving to Boston?" She asked. "Was it because I'd been talking about moving there?" It was true that she had talked about moving again, now that she had graduated college, but she was still job searching and living with her friends, and I had been trying to detach myself from being on her case too much. With a part-time job and new friends in Providence she was having a new beginning. I assured her that my decision to come to Boston had nothing to do with her, but that I too needed a new beginning.

"I just want you to try to understand…I'm not asking you to take sides, but just to allow Peter and I do what we have to do." I pleaded.

"But why? Why did you leave?" Sophie whined.

"It's complicated, honey." I paused.

"That's trite" she said, as I could hear a long sigh.

Then she whispered: "I'm sorry…really, I am. But I don't get it. You were perfect parents, we had a perfect life. It just doesn't make sense." I could hear the sob in her voice. I could hear the guilt in mine.

"Sophie, let's just say, he wasn't there for me when I most needed him—that's why I left. We've been growing apart, I promise to explain later." Explanations would have to wait till we could sit and talk face to face; till I could make it better for her.

"When can we get together?" I asked.

Silence. Sophie's phone started beeping with another call coming in..."I don't know. I've got to go, Mom....take care of yourself. Talk later—"

"I love you" I yelled, as the call ended abruptly.

Chapter 3

"I wish that life should not be cheap, but sacred... the days to be as centuries, loaded, fragrant." Ralph Waldo Emerson

To: Kendra@gmail.com

Subject: Finally!

It was so good to hear from you and to know that the first draft of the "Saturn Book" I attached in the other email is helping you a bit. I'm sorry it's taken me so long to respond to your last email, but I've been almost too exhausted to write. Now I finally have time to send you "news" of what's been happening, and...if you don't mind, instead of journal writing this morning, I'll ramble on a bit with you....

I just finished moving all my stuff. Within a couple of weeks, I was able to clean and paint, and clean and paint... sigh. What a job. It felt endless, but it's done now. Peter didn't want to have anything to do with my project. (That's what he calls this move....I don't think he gets it.) And I was able to furnish the small rooms here with furniture from home. Peter became "conveniently" away at another conference last week. And since I won't need a car here I only took what I loved and really needed. The rest I left for Peter...besides he wasn't moving, and we're not divorced, at least not yet.

I must admit I've been fighting off feeling terribly lonely. Both Peter and Sophie are upset with me obviously, and their way of dealing with me is to not talk. I understand, and I don't understand. It's all okay I guess…all things "in the right time"?

But—it's good to finally feel "nested" here in this new place and thanks for being so patient with me. I can't always write. People think I'm an extrovert—that persona mask—but sometimes I have to struggle to even pick up the phone or write an email. Anyway, here's what's been happening~

On Thursday I brought my old Larkin desk here—with the help of the movers—and placed it opposite the paned window that looks out onto the street. When we brought the desk in, I placed a photo of Peter and Sophie on the top, but then tears filled my eyes again and sadness melted into the quietness of the room. So I tucked away the photos into a drawer of the desk.

Do you know these old desks? I love these Victorian writing desks with their secret drawers and nooks in it. When I opened it up for the first time this morning I saw that I had a little box with rosary beads from Assisi, and some Easter incense from a trip Peter and I once took to Greece. There was a pack of Tarot Cards still hidden in a drawer and a black and white photo of my parents when they were first married.

And then, in one of the 'secret nooks' I saw a piece of yellowed linen—I don't remember ever seeing it before! But as I unwrapped it, I saw a "hand-rolled joint" in it—this must have been from so long ago I don't even remember…anyway, I flushed it down the toilet, thinking how it was the last remnant of my "hippie" years here in Boston. Now that drawer is empty.

But on the desktop I put my green fountain pen (not that I use it!), my leather journal, an antique copper astroglobe (with astrology symbols on it) and a little stained glass lamp...a few special things to warm the room and my heart.

I remember that they used to call these small writing desks "Larkin desks" because they were bought with coupons by Victorian ladies who had collected enough Larkin Soap to buy one cheap. Can you imagine? I bought it for $400 when I first moved to the hill right after college.

I think of this room as a sanctuary—it's small, but the high ceilings give me a sense of spaciousness and the dark rose painted walls seem to "hold me." I guess that's a strange thing to say about a room, rather than a person. Then I put two comfy rocking chairs with olive green cushions, facing each other with a small table between them, and placed my favorite amber stained glass lamp between them.

The amber light casts a soft glow around the room, but I've yet to find the quiet moments when I actually use my old pen and journal. I put a large dark wood bookcase next to the desk (so many books I couldn't leave behind!) and at least a dozen journals I've kept through the years. And then there are all the boxes of photographs upstairs. Some things I never throw out...

The only thing that doesn't fit into the ambience of the room is the computer, but I must have it for the astrology programs and my emailing. I've faced it next to the old desk opposite the window and street so I can look out and watch the people walking by...I guess this room must once have been a shop.

And then I hung my grandmother's painting of the "Fortune Teller" above the fireplace. I couldn't help but feel that she would be happy I wanted her to be here with me in some way. This painting brings a bit of her into my life—I wonder if her spirit could benevolently care for me? I certainly feel I need all the help I can get—and if it's from the "ancestors" that's even better...

Anyway, since I'm looking at it now, let me see if I can describe it a bit...it's signed: Elizabeth English, 1904. Peter once described it as a Rembrandt-like painting—a painting that hints of a story—the story of a fortune teller reading the tea leaves of a fashionable lady at the turn of the century. It's large and blackish, and as you look beyond the layers of paint, you can see the darkened room of a woman holding a tea cup, and a lady having her fortune told. It has a rather large gold frame and fits perfectly above the fireplace mantel. My mother once said that my grandmother painted it when she was twenty four years old and living with her aunt at 33 Joy Street on Beacon Hill just before she married. It was the last painting she ever did—and then she married, had five children, and never painted again.

❧

So Kendra, are you doing charts of people you know? It's a great way to learn astrology. But sometimes I don't know if it's more disturbing or comforting to look at the charts of people you love. Mom, for example, is now 88 years old as of last Jan 1st and she is in her Third Saturn Return! Saturn has returned to the same place in her chart as when she was first born. Yes, there really is such a thing as a third return, but not much is written about it, because at 88...well, what can I say?

But for Mom at 88, her third Saturn Return has "played out" by having a stroke. And now that I'm in Boston, I visit her every morning in the nursing home. It's hard to see such an independent woman being so confined. Her loneliness and my loneliness feels almost infectious at times, and yet I must go see her—last week I fed her spoonfuls of pumpkin pie and ice cream and she loved it. She feels like my child now.

I wonder about her stroke, I wonder too about her "transiting Uranus" on her Moon—a fitting example of a Uranian shock, this stroke. Her semi-paralysis and restriction in the nursing home is echoed in that placement of transiting Saturn being in the "12th house"—that's the section of the chart that rules hospitals and confinement, among other things. The Saturnian feeling of solitariness seems fitting for the charts—yet it all makes me sad. I don't know if it's easier or harder not having brothers or sisters at times like this, but it seems more poignant at times to be alone.

Can I share something with you? If you were here with me now, I'd tell you about a particular time; a day that was a half-remembered dream when I was very young. I remember these Sunday afternoons as if they were a patchwork quilt. Every Sunday it was a ritual to spend time with my grandmother, my aunt and uncle. Those Sundays were a patchwork: crisp November twigs snapping under my feet, cold cheeks and frozen

mittens warming near the kerosene heater, glimpses of oil paintings examined through the haze of my uncle's cigarette smoke.

My aunt and uncle lived in a tiny "Quonset house" tucked away high on a hill with a view of the Connecticut River. After we managed to walk the hill to their house, we would go for long rambling walks in the afternoons, sometimes for picnics or ice-skating, sometimes just to walk their dog, Teddy, who I was allowed to lead on a leash. We would explore the woods and abandoned summer cottages down by the railroad tracks alongside the river, and I would collect rocks and leaves for science class, and sometimes we would find old magazines and fragments of antiques from the attics of the abandoned houses.

Some Sundays we'd go in search of daguerreotypes, which we would buy for 50 cents from part-time antique dealers who would open their homes on week-ends for Sunday lookers. These daguerreotypes were tiny hard-covered books, which when opened, revealed photographs encased in gold veneer and velvet, taken roughly one-hundred years ago. There we would discover pictures of Civil War heroes and children too cumbersomely dressed to smile. When we got the photos back to my aunt's house we'd pry open the backs and look for bits of old love letters, locks of hair, or newspaper clippings from that time.

Then it would be time to feed little Teddy, and I would watch as my aunt crushed up little oat-meal bars and carefully mixed them with the meaty dog food. She seemed to know what was best for her little dog. My uncle would then cook up a hearty, and usually too spicy meal, after which there would be a few sprinklings of good-humored criticism from my mother, who was not one to use onions, garlic, and anything more potent than a pinch of salt.

And there sitting on the sofa was my grandmother; Elizabeth. I can still see the paisley shawl she wore and the sofa where she would sit on, quiet and untouched. I wonder if her children made her happy; I wonder why she had five children and gave up her painting? I remember her sitting under the last oil painting she made: The Fortune Teller. I have it now in my study, and am amused that I have become, in some ways, the fortune teller. But if my grandmother was around now I would ask her what she thought when she looked at that last painting? If she were here I would ask her if she was pleased with her fortune—had she been generous enough with herself? Had she been giving enough to her children? I will never know.

That's the way it was then....but after dinner, we'd be full and tired, and taking a flash light we'd make our way through the darkness down the unpaved road to our car. The stars seemed so close and brilliant on those nights! As we rode home I would nestle my head against my mother's soft beaver coat, and listen to the comedy of "Jack Benny and Rochester" on the car radio.

I'll never know what my grandmother was really like; I only know the mixed joys and sorrows of the family karmic inheritance that has been handed down to me. I love what Longfellow once wrote: "If we could read the secret history of our families, we would find in each man's life a sorrow and a suffering enough to disarm all hostility" I think he actually said "enemies" rather than "families" but it works either way, doesn't it? Enough for now, dear Kendra, thanks for listening.

Fondly,

Isabelle~

Chapter 4

"Amor Fati: The Love of One's Fate"

I turned off the computer. And then I sat, and noticed what I hadn't seen before—the cobwebs and daddy-long-legs that hung around the ceilings, and the little flies that swarmed and hung around the window panes. It was going to be ceaseless battle with them and they certainly didn't feel like a good omen. I wondered if the flies were coming from the back of the fireplace and if they had something to do with bad karma left behind by previous owners. No, that's too superstitious.

But this morning as I sat there looking out through the panes in the old window, I noted the plight of a trapped fly caught in the corner by a near-by spider. So what to do—save the fly or kill them both? I was reaching for a broom to swat them when I saw a man's face looking in at me—no, he wasn't looking at me, he was staring at the face engraved on the fireplace cover. I shot a glance at the closed eyes of the Goddess on the fireplace and then back at the stranger's wide eyes. They were that pale shade of blue that suggested either innocence or cold detachment.

Theo, my short-haired prince of a cat brushed up against me, curling his tail protectively around my leg. I reached down and held him to my chest like a shield. I didn't move, in fact I froze. But then the man's eyes caught mine; he had me cornered. He looked like a picture I had seen of the artist Monet, with his wide broad-brimmed hat pulled low over his forehead, accentuating his eyes and neatly trimmed beard.

I took a deep breath and lowered Theo to the floor. I needed to move out of the reclusive mode I had been taking refuge in, and so I opened the door. "Hello...." I said as I put on a smile and extended my hand. He tipped his floppy hat and put his large hand in mine.

"I'm sorry; I don't mean to disturb you. I was just admiring your fireplace. It's lovely." He had a kind voice.

"Well thank you." We both turned to look at the goddess' noble face. "Yes, she's why I'm here. Goddesses have a certain compelling power, don't you think?"

"I do" he said, turning his head around and sweeping in the full extent of the room. He then looked back at me.

"Yes, she's got such a serene expression on her face—I see her as being like Hestia, guardian of the Hearth."

"Really? I thought she might be St. Bridget. Excuse me for not introducing myself, I'm Thomas."

"Isabelle. Isabelle Cocroft. And is it Thomas or Tomas? Unusual, the way you pronounce it...."

"Well, it's Irish. It's an old Gaelic name. You can call me Thomas without the accent. I don't mean to sound pretentious or anything."

"No, you don't. Come in..." He certainly looked Irish with his ruddy complexion, and I could see that one of his eyes was milky, as if a film covered it. I would have guessed that he was blind in that eye, but obviously he could see well enough to spot me, and his single eye seemed to take everything in the room. He was also carrying a loose shoulder bag with several books stuffed in it.

"So what will you be doing in this fine room, Isabelle?"

"Counseling. Astrology." I paused. It always takes a moment for people to digest the second part.

"Astrology? Don't know if I exactly believe in it myself, but I find it fascinating. I used to be a social worker though I don't do that work anymore."

"Why not? Are you retired?" He struck me as the kind of person who liked walking around the hill and talking to strangers and shop keepers. An extroverted introvert, if there was such a thing.

"Yes, retired from being a "professional rescuer"—social worker. Now I have a little second hand bookstore over here on Chestnut Street. You must come visit. We'll be neighbors now." He grinned widely.

"Well come in then, and visit for a moment, if you like..." I pointed to the two rockers.

"Can't say I haven't got the time, 'cause I do." When he came closer I could smell pipe smoke. I looked down, and saw that he was wearing black cowboy boots. So much for the artist, Monet, I thought, I shouldn't be so quick to try to 'peg' people.

"Sit down," I said, pointing again to the chairs. "And if you want to have a smoke, it's OK…really."

"You don't miss much, do you? Guess I must smell a bit like an ole geezer." He laughed without smiling this time and gently lifted Theo off the chair. Pulling out a well-used pipe he lit up the bowl with some tobacco from his pocket and turned his gaze on me. The first whiff of smoke was sweet.

"Your goddess here looks like a virgin goddess; a woman who was "one-unto herself as they'd say." He took a deep inhale, exhale, and then took off his hat like he had forgotten for a moment. His hair was mostly white and quite thick. "So tell me Isabelle, why would someone want to know their future anyway?"

"I don't know; I don't do that. I don't tell futures exactly, I try to inspire people by looking at who they are through their charts…through the symbolism I see there. I can see repeating patterns and something of the story that they tell about themselves. I try to help them look at their stories and reframe them so they can see new possibilities that are a little different, so they make better decisions."

"Well that's a refreshing take on that! Never thought of it that way." Thomas looked up at the cobweb I hadn't touched and I felt embarrassed.

"Sometimes it's just a way for people to talk about what's happening in their lives without...pathologizing it. You know what I mean? Without judgment being put on them. But I've never wanted to know too much of what might happen...I believe more in free will than predictions." I paused.

I could see he wore a thin chain around his neck holding what looked to be a Celtic cross on it. I looked down and fingered the tiny gold-chain bracelet that Peter had given me. I had never taken it off.

Theo suddenly jumped into my lap and nudged me out of my short reverie. "I guess some people would say it's ridiculous or arrogant to try to read the mind of God this way. But it's a lot about sacred geometry, and the charts are like deciphering puzzles...I love doing them."

"Sounds like you also like to dwell in the underworlds of the psyche." He looked me straight in the eye.

I didn't flinch. "I like to explore mysteries—not crimes, but real mysteries...the big questions, like life direction and soul purpose."

"Ah, then you must come to our Sunday Afternoon Philosopher's Club! That's just what we do there. Actually we mostly just talk, share books...a little "mind stimulation" over a cup of caffeine. Think you'd like that?"

"Of course, I would. I love books...and journaling. And I'm writing a book." I laughed at my audaciousness of telling this to a stranger. "Well, I'm trying to write a book—it's a struggle."

"Really...on what?"

"Astrology. On Saturn Returns—those times of initiation and crisis we all go through when we're around the ages of 29 and 59. I'm sure you remember your first Saturn Return at 29, and now—well, you look a little like the old wise man himself, ole Saturn Returning." I grinned at him wondering if he looked more like Santa Claus than Monet.

I couldn't believe I said all that. Why was I saying all this to a stranger? Was I trying to impress him? I crossed my legs, looked down at my soft gray sweater and stroked the wool, as if to soothe myself. Then I gave Theo a long smooth stroke which made him stand straight up, tail high.

Thomas took a thoughtful inhale of smoke, and I watched the long exhale. He looked quietly around the room. I didn't mind his quietness, and his interiority or silence was actually rather pleasing, but I wanted to know more: "So, are you a Christian? I like your Celtic Cross...." I asked

"No—yes, no labels please...it's all good. For me, life is like one of those psychological Rorschach ink-blot tests—you know you get back what you see. Do you know what I mean? It's all a mess of crazy lines unless it's a projection of what's in here." He pointed to his heart.

I liked that. "And what's in there?" I pointed my finger to his heart, raising my eyebrows. Thomas attempted a little smile and coughed.

"Have you ever had your chart done?" I asked.

"No. Might you be offering to do mine?"

"We could. I do what is called Jungian Astrology, or archetypal astrology. Did you know that Carl Jung used astrology with his clients? And his work on synchronicity, meaningful coincidences, is what this work is based on as far as I'm concerned." My arms swept towards the bookcase.

"I see." He looked thoughtful. "I have a whole section of his books in the bookshop too. You should come by and check them out! I think you'd like them—lots of inspiration, art, biographies and psychology. My place isn't much larger than your space here."

I nodded. I've always loved bookstores despite the fact I spend so much time on the computer. "I'd love to come visit...and you know, you'll only believe in astrology or not if you have your chart done. It's not so much about theory, but about the process. It either works for you or doesn't."

"Would you like to do my chart?" He asked, raising his eyebrows and leaning towards me. I could see that this was a heartfelt invitation.

"I could. I would....but it's also how I earn my living, so I'd need to charge you unless we're just chatting. Or...maybe we could exchange some books for a reading?" I asked.

"Good idea." Thomas had an intensity that shot forth from his one eye. The other eye was not for the world to know about. He could change his manner in an instant, and he looked as if he was deeply rooted to something within himself. Simply said, he had charisma.

Suddenly I felt defensive. Or was it shyness? We both stood up at the same time, as if we knew our time was up for the moment. I wanted to add more, but what? Suddenly I burst out with what I was afraid was too much: "This kind of astrology helps us feel part of a larger pattern of things...in a way, it's a spiritual language...and when you sense the astrological weather of the time, you feel a bit more....in control."

"In control?" He laughed.

"You know—did you ever read the formula about fate and free will and character in old esoteric books? The one that says that: Fate + Character = destiny."

"Hermes Tresmigistus. Yes! I remember reading about that—from that old tome, The Emerald Tablet, or something like that?"

"Right—good memory!" I was surprised he knew that. Ah...a worthy opponent in matters of the mind.

"So I was born March 28th—well, here, I'll write it all down on this paper for you. Place too, right? Born in Gloucester, Massachusetts. How about tomorrow, then—same time?" He handed me a little paper he ripped out of his notebook with his birth information on it, and we said our goodbyes. I was happy to have my first friend here....and a "Philosopher's Club" too? It felt good to make a connection.

❧

And so I met Thomas. After he left I began working on his chart, taking it one step at a time, like doing a puzzle. Aries Sun, Cancer Moon, with Scorpio rising. It felt good to do the familiar circling round the chart, lines and arrows, and little stars reminding me of what to say, what not to forget.

And then the next morning, I worked on it a little more before going through more unpacking and discarding of boxes, purging myself of what I didn't need any more. It seemed as if a space was beginning to open within me, a space for the future to come into...a space that went beyond my fear of any prediction coming true.

Chapter 5

"All changes, even the most longed for, have their melancholy; for what we leave behind us is a part of ourselves; we must die to one life before we can enter another. ~Anatole France

The next morning as I was preparing for my reading for Thomas, I couldn't stop thinking about meeting Peter for the first time, in this very same room, so many years ago. When I first met Peter I believed in predictions. I took life more literally. And that day felt uncannily similar to yesterday's meeting with Thomas—it was that same sense that something was happening in this meeting that was larger than me, than us.

Finally, I stopped all my nervous preparations for Thomas's reading, sat down, and let myself remember that day…but I couldn't really remember. It was all a pleasant blur.

Then I remembered my journals! The one crazy thing I had done in making this move to Boston was to take along all my photograph albums and all my journals—there was a stack next to my bed upstairs—there must have been close to twenty journals! And I remembered I wrote a very long and detailed journal entry that day, but I didn't remember what I said. Maybe I could find it.

I went to the bookshelf and sifted through the musty journals. All those years….and there it was—! The one for that year, 1977….. I opened it and began to read:

September 30, 1977

What a day today! I don't know what to make of this—??! Before Peter arrived I had been crying. Peter was my only client today, and I was standing at the window before he came, my eyes glistening with tears, listening to Bonnie Raitt sing: "Love Has No Pride." Something was shifting within me—that longing for love that's been so heavy on my heart these days is almost unendurable. And….I can no longer stand for "pretense" any longer—not in myself or anyone else.

Maybe I have no more pride, or shame. Nothing to hide, nothing to pretend. As I listened to Bonnie's poignant song, I could feel her words penetrating past all of my usual defenses. I'm ready for a change.

This is my first Saturn Return. Twenty nine years old, and maybe fated to be single forever. Who knows? I know they say these are times of rough waters. Never an easy passage, yet being with Peter this morning, it was clear just how vulnerable and insecure I am, and how much I'm in need of connection and reassurance. This is a secret I try to keep from others, and I know it's not good to keep up false pride.

It was just after ten o'clock. I looked at the clock and wondered if he'd be late. And then I saw him right there—he was standing at the door, knocking. I quickly turned off the music, wiped my eyes, and wondered how I was going to be able to do a "reading" in such a state of mind.

As I opened the door I was taken aback by Peter's stunning presence. Long dark hair, pale white skin and near-black eyes framed a nearly impeccable face, hinting of some purity of heart. I knew he was twenty nine years old, yet he seemed older than his years...a certain quietness seemed to permeate him. He was coming here today for his first astrology reading, and as he extended his hand, I was impressed by the gracious formality of his handshake.

"Good to meet you Peter." I took his hand in mine. We paused in silence, waiting for the other to speak first.

"I'm Isabelle. Come in...is this your first reading?" I asked while motioning him into my little room.

"It is...and what a lovely place you have here!" His eyes swept up to the high ceilings and across the dark wooden walls and landed on the fireplace. "Is that a Goddess face carved into the fireplace?" He stared intently at her face while I stared at his. He was tall and thin, and wore a dark navy pea-coat with the collar turned up around his neck.

"Yes, I think she is...I'm not sure..." I answered, while motioning him to sit at the counseling table. I had hoped that the goddess's numinous face would bring the spirit of the feminine into the consulting room, as her downward looking eyes seemed to know how to keep a secret. She would stay in the shadows and never speak of nuances of mood or mind...

The two chairs were facing each other, looking as if they were waiting for us, and the moody light poured through the windows casting shadows. I hoped Peter wasn't put off by the Victorian and yet rather intimate setting of the room.

"So have you been doing this long?" He asked. "It's my first time—you know—-I don't even come up to Boston very much. But there's no one in Newport that does this...and I thought it might help..."

"Of course it's fine!" I said.

"You know, I could tell from talking with you yesterday that you take this seriously, you're not just a—what do you call them—a 'sun-sign' astrologer or a sketchy fortune teller. I like that...I like your connection with Jung and that you're a therapist as well. "He sat down slowly.

I nodded and looked down. I hoped I could give him what he wanted. I do take this work very seriously but I don't like making people nervous. Don't like making myself nervous either.

"Let's just see what we can find here that could be helpful to you" I grinned and splayed the charts in my hand like a card deck. "I don't predict death by execution or anything like that—but who knows what we'll see....we'll just read what's here."

He didn't know that he was actually one of my first paying clients, though I had been doing charts for years. I hoped I could do a good job; I hoped I could give him what he needed to hear, I hoped I could act like a conduit for something larger than myself.

It was so quiet for a moment. I could hear the pendulum on the clock moving, and I wondered if I had remembered to clear the clutter of papers and coffee mugs off my desk. He looked instead at the bookshelf which covered one wall.

"Lovely room," he whispered, "I like all your books." And I admired the pristine clarity of his English accent.

Most of us don't like to feel too vulnerable, and though we don't want to admit it, I think there's a mutual resonance that happens when we either like or dislike another person or situation—it's uncanny when it's almost instantaneous. I could feel a warm resonance happening, yet I wondered if he saw me as a quaint oddity, something left over from the era of Charles Dickens—a mood that Beacon Hill seemed to resonate with.

Peter had called the day before saying that he was coming to me because he liked the tiny advertisement for my services in "Boston This Week" which noted my background in psychology—specifically, the psychology of Carl Jung, who had used astrology in his work and who—Peter said he knew—that Jung was the first to give astrology and world of the unconscious, a serious confirmation.

I remember after I hung up the phone thinking that here was a gentle man who had come to yet another turning point in his life, and who probably simply needed a little psychic cheerleading. I knew he was a potter from Newport, Rhode Island, and working down on a shop by the waterfront. That was all he had said over the phone

It's easy to see most things without even looking at a chart, as emotions are revealed on our faces more than we'd like to imagine. Most of us have no idea how transparent we are—nor do we want to admit that everything about us speaks to who we are—not just our clothes or our tone of voice, but even the way we look at each other, or don't look, or the way the jaw muscle can be seen tightening or the twitching of the nose. All this can reveal almost as much as the astrological chart. Peter's eyes looked soft and curious.

The flesh and blood reality of a client always shocks me at first, because after spending several hours analyzing their charts, I think I know them, and I don't. Clients never seem to look as I would imagine them, and it's humbling to be so often wrong about first impressions from the chart. I see the wounds and struggle first—the squares and oppositions that leap off the page, and I'm awed to hear how courageously they've survived and thrived, even under the worst combination of aspects. Peter had one of those "challenging" birth charts, but he appeared to be a survivor, and had somehow learned to thrive despite having what the ancient astrologers used to call '"malefic" aspects. Of course, I never use those words, malefic or auspicious, but I couldn't help but wonder what kind of wounding this man had survived. His chart was challenging, yet his eyes were kind.

And so I began the reading in my usual manner: "The birth chart is like a conference table, and the planets circling around it are like the different parts of your Self sitting around the table. The Sun is the chairperson and represents your basic identity, the Moon reflects your emotional nature, the Rising sign is your sign that was rising at the moment of your birth, and reflects your style of "moving-out" into the world, and the Nodes are about your life direction and soul purpose. The lines crossing in the center of the chart connect all this—all these voices in our psyche, all these aspects—they show where one's inner conversation is divided against itself, or where it's aligned or flowing.... "

My voice trailed off as I looked up at Peter. I wanted to see if he understood what I was saying or if he was resisting this information. There were lots of "squared aspects" in his chart, suggesting that he was being pulled in different directions, and that his inner dialogue was tense and paradoxical. I felt like I was looking into an open wound and I hoped he wasn't flinching.

"So if the chart is like a conference table, then the chairperson for you is represented by your Sun sign, Virgo, which is another way to say that you have a natural inclination to analyze, to help others, and to see the possibilities of the Ideal. But Virgo can be an exacting and tough taskmaster when he wants—it's not an easy Sign to be born under, in fact, it's probably the most misunderstood sign of the zodiac. Yet your Moon, your emotional nature, is in Pisces reflecting the Soul of a poet, mystic or dreamer..."

I had worn my blue jeans, cowboy boots, and black turtleneck that day. I smiled at him, wishing I was talking to him over a "Neptunian" glass of wine rather than over a pile of charts.

I stared back down at his charts....blankly. There was so much to say, yet the words didn't come. Silence is fine, I thought, he can see I'm contemplating the chart—but what was this internal sabotage I began feeling within me? Beginners mind, I thought. But do I know what I'm doing? This is so much harder than traditional psychotherapy; I ought to be using my counseling degree instead of doing this! How much easier it is when the client does most of the talking…and, I reminded myself, how important it was to get "me" out of the way so I could be a conduit for what needs to be said. But the words simply weren't coming. Beginner's mind, I thought… beginner's mind.

And so I stumbled on: "When I look at a chart, I see things in terms of reincarnation, karma, and of life lessons moving through this life and past lives—I hope that way of seeing things doesn't offend you—"

"Oh no, I accept reincarnation as a possibility—I just don't know, but go on…it feels right so far." I could see that Peter was not only allowing himself to have a reading, but he was willing to "let me in" as well. But I needed to be careful. We were coming to the more challenging parts of his chart, and I didn't want to scare him or be too harsh. I wondered too if I sometimes pretended too much false optimism.

"So do you see these "squares" from the Sun and Moon to Uranus, and to the North Node? Uranus is the planet of rebellion, uniqueness, and independence. The squares suggest an inner struggle that most people won't see in you at first—a struggle to do things your own way, to go against the grain at times. This kind of independence can be perceived as indifference or coldness." I lifted my eyebrows as if to question if this was true, but he didn't say anything. I was puzzled by his chart; I had an image of a beautiful earthenware pot with a slight crack in it.

But then I pulled myself back and went on: "And yet, this is how it should be—because your guiding North Star, the

"North Node" is next to, or "conjunct" Uranus, implying that you are the kind of person who is often called to take the road less traveled...as they used to say."

Peter nodded and smiled. Perhaps my words sounded a bit cliché, but I had to start easy and "feel into" how much he really wanted to hear. His chart echoed his personal manner: a warm, skeptical and private sort of man. He had his Venus in the intense sign of Scorpio, but this was softened by his dreamy Pisces Moon in the 12th house of the unconscious.

Peter knew he had come to a turning point in his life, and I could see that by looking at his transits too. I didn't know the story of his life, but from looking at the planets that were currently transiting across the heavens and in his chart, I suspected his life was being turned upside down now. He too was having the "Saturn Return." Others might simply call it a major first life crisis, or the time when tough decisions get to be made.

And then there were those "opportunities for love" that were transiting across his chart now—those astrological aspects between Venus and Jupiter. These usually predict an opportunity for a love relationship to happen—Venus representing the relationship and Jupiter the realm of many opportunities. I had no idea how he would play them out in his life, but I was beginning to wonder.

We talked for almost two hours. I could see that here was someone who wanted me to re-affirm for him what he already knew to be true—-that his first marriage was over, and the chance for love was still on the horizon. I hinted of that, but he didn't respond to my hint of approaching love. What he did say, at the end of our session, was that he'd like to come back.

As soon as he left I walked over to my "private papers" and pulled out my chart. I wanted to see what the interplay of our two charts looked like together. I wondered if there were any signs that suggested that his Venus/Jupiter transit might involve me. Was there a hint of destiny here? He was a Virgo and I'm a Libra, an earth sign and an air sign.

I don't know. I believe in this language, and yet it's like a finger pointing at the moon! It doesn't get you there. Instead it describes the journey and though I can make it sound comforting for others, I can't do that for myself. The "road map" of astrology gives some people a feeling of control or security, but I feel...more like a reluctant astrologer. I don't want to see too much. I like seeing possibilities and inspiring others. That's it.

It's true in love relationships the fire signs—Aries, Leo and Sagittarius—tend to get along best with the air signs—Gemini, Libra and Aquarius—and earth signs, like Taurus, Virgo, and Capricorn are compatible with the water signs of Cancer, Scorpio and Pisces, but it gets so complicated with the Moon and Rising signs! If one person's Sun sign is the same as your Moon or Rising Sign, that's a prediction of compatibility as well. So....what does that mean???

I put the journal down. That was the end of the entry that day. I could see how my writing changed from neatly written script to a fast slanted emotional outpouring. I actually had used one of those fountains pens that were so popular back then, and the writing was smudgy at times.

Ah—-Peter and I have a lot of "grit as well as grace" in our charts. In our combined charts, in the synastry, there was a strong and strange blend of signs and aspects. But did it matter? I pushed my chair back, put down the old journal, and walked over to the same window and stared through the glass. The late afternoon sunlight was making moving shadows and patterns over everything. The seasons were finally changing. Then I rummaged through my old CD's and listened again to Bonnie sing "Love has no pride" What does that mean for me now? Is there such a thing as "amor fati" or love at first sight, or fated love? I didn't know then and I don't know now.

Chapter 6

"When an inner situation is not made conscious, it happens outside as fate." Carl Jung

I was still rereading my old journal when Thomas arrived for his "reading." I had been up since 6:00 am working on his chart, so I felt prepared even though I had allowed myself to drift off so deeply into my journal…into my private papers. I quickly slipped the journal onto my desk and answered the door. He looked exactly the same, except this time he had a black jacket on over his simple shirt and blue jeans.

As he sat down I noticed he still had a pipe in the pocket of his jacket, so I offered to let him smoke again, as I truly liked the smell of pipe smoke. He was pleased, and as he sank into his seat and lit his pipe, he seemed prepared to be amused if nothing else.

I was prepared for this reading, and yet I can never tell how a session will unfold—sometimes it appears to be an easy read and then turns out to be much more complex than anticipated.

"So Thomas, I like to think of astrology as being "the positive contemplation of change" and try to keep my readings in that tone, but what we'll want to do to start is to look at your life, your history in light of the symbolism I see here."

I saw him nod in agreement, but all I could think of was how this reading was going to be a challenge for me. Thomas's forthright Aries Sun was squared by illusory Neptune. This man could be steeped in illusions about himself. I puzzled about how to describe his moody Cancer Moon that was conjunct, or "cuddling up" with the mythological Pluto, Lord of the Underworld. It also had a tense challenging square to Saturn.

"So…one has to tread lightly on the astrological chart—just as one must tread lightly when reviewing one's life, eh?" Shame and pride are so intertwined, and astrologers must walk a fine line: how to be bold enough to talk of light and shadow, strength and weakness, good and not-so-good. Clients often assume we see or know more than we do, and that's enough to make anyone nervous. But Thomas didn't seem nervous.

"OK…" Now how can one word sound so skeptical?

I began: "When a soul chooses to be born with an Aries Sun, they want to learn courage. And to learn courage one needs to take risks, to feel the fear and do it anyway. So with your Aries Sun you're a survivor, a pioneer, and one who is usually open to new experiences, and often volunteers to be first in line. In Tarot, Aries is like the first card of the Fool or the young man who is taking off on a new adventure with knapsack on his back. He thrives on new beginnings, and seeing life like a journey."

"Oh yes, I think of myself as 'the Fool on the Hill' like in the old Beatles song. Remember that?"

"I do. And yet I see you as being a wise man too—there's an acceptance about the 'wise old fool' isn't there—we're all quite paradoxical, aren't we? But for you, these courageous new beginnings are probably more stressful than people might realize—people who don't know you very well probably see you as strong and confident most of the time." I looked over at him for confirmation, but he wore a poker face.

I took my pen and pointed to the Moon on his chart. "The stress arises more from your private emotional nature, that changing Cancer Moon, which is much more introverted and moody in nature than your Aries Sun sign, and being next to Pluto, the invisible god of the Underworld, the Moon/Pluto combination suggests that you're more comfortable not being exposed. You're more likely to be the one helping or nurturing the other person while keeping the focus off yourself. Yes?"

That comment cracked open his poker face just enough. "But I'm here, aren't I? Being exposed?" We laughed.

"Yes, you're being brave, acting on your Aries Sun now, but that Moon in Cancer and your Scorpio rising doesn't like to be too vulnerable or exposed.... but it hints that you are very curious, a little intense, maybe secretive? But we need to go deeper."

His boot started twitching a little, as he took a deep inhale. The pungent sweet smoke filled the room.

"Go on, you're doing good. I can take it." We both laughed.

"Well, like me, you've got a family karmic inheritance to deal with, and I'd say it's probably more intense from your Mother's side of your family. It would have been a strong karmic relationship with her, though not always easy. She probably was too controlling for you, and because of the Moon's conjunction to Pluto, I suspect there was something deeply missing in that relationship. She gave you the love she had, but it may have been missing a lot."

He didn't say a thing, but his lower lip hinted at a pout. I went on: "Although with Neptune in the 4rd house "squaring off" to your Sun…well, that 4th house represents your parents and early home, and a square is a challenging aspect. Now with Neptune…Neptune rules over the ocean, spirituality, and….spirits. Was your father an alcoholic or not there for you in some important way?" That was a leap, but I wanted to try.

"You got it; he was both. And you're right about her as well." He seemed pleased with my success.

My eyes swept around the chart again. "You've got some things here—this Cancer Moon conjunct Pluto—that suggests your childhood was rather difficult, and that your mother could have had a manipulative effect on you. Perhaps that relationship was—-"

"Yeah, yeah, that's why I became a social worker—she liked the idea of me saving people, and then I liked the idea of being a bookstore owner…to figure it all out.

I love people and books. Mom was fine." He coughed and knocked the ashes out of his pipe and started a refill. "My childhood was mixed, but with my blind eye the other kids saw me as being different and that didn't help. So Mom tried to help or intervene for me. I was painfully shy as a kid, and she was always breaking up fights between me and the other kids."

"Perhaps she took center stage for a long time—even up to your Saturn Return at age twenty-nine? Did things change then? They usually do..."

"Yes, I had been studying for the priesthood—another idea of my mother's actually, and it was around that time that I became disillusioned with the church—just before I was ordained. It was a shock to her—- she never understood. I took a little time off, and then did some things and then went on towards getting my social work degree. It was a rough road for an Irish Catholic kid."

"I bet it was." There were some real issues around illusion and disillusion in that Sun/Neptune aspect. Cancers like the idea of family and being financially secure.

"I was married for a while and worked as a social worker with kids—the really gritty kind of social work with abused boys. Then my wife inherited some money, so we didn't have to depend on my money, and we didn't have any kids of our own. Oh, I was quite an oddball, even back then."

I waited to see if he'd explain more, but he didn't, so I went on: "Now this Moon/Pluto in the sign of Cancer could give you empathy and an understanding of "the shadow" that Carl Jung wrote about so much—yes?—the dark side of poverty and underworld that those boys lived in…."

He nodded in agreement.

"But what happened with your wife…..did you leave her? I see a lot of change in your chart around the age of forty-one, at your 'Uranus Opposition.' You know, everyone has a Uranus Oppositon at around age forty when there's a great urge to do something different because we realize we're running out of time. And our psyche wants to pick up on forgotten dreams, or simply stop doing what it doesn't want to do anymore. It can be a rebellious time." I could only see the symbolic language of his life and could only guess how he played these aspects out in his life.

"Yes, that was the time we split up. Confusing time. I wasn't good for anything at that point, kind of had a breakdown and honestly, I just wanted out. I miss her though, now…sometimes. She remarried right away." I could see the subtle cloud of sadness move over him, as he turned away.

What a good man, I thought; what a decent person he seemed to be. "Yet with all that Cancer in your chart did you ever feel that part of you was like Peter Pan and never wanted to grow up? You know…kind of a 'puer' as the psychologists say…"

"Oh yeah, my wife hated how I resisted everything...even her, at times. It was hard for me to commit to anything even when I was committed." Just then the desk phone rang, and the answering machine loudly interrupted:

"Hello, you've reached Isabelle, at Priorities Astrological Counseling. I'm either with a client or out of the office so please leave your number and I'll call you back." The caller hung up. It felt a little embarrassing. "Let's go on...sorry."

I picked up Thomas's other chart—his current transit charts for the year ahead, and looked at what I had circled in red. "These charts give a kind of 'weather-forecast' of the year ahead—-I don't like to think of it as prediction, but more like a weather forecast of the time....and you've got a couple of storms here, and shifting high and low pressure systems."

"I should hope I have a few. Wouldn't want to bore you!" As he laughed I noticed his teeth were stained from his pipe. It didn't bother me as his smile stretched from one side of his face to the other, and cracked open his face into such innocence. There was charisma there. I wondered if he knew it.

"You don't bore me." In fact, I was beginning to feel the warmth of whatever that unknown quality of charisma is—that charm. I lost my trail of thoughts for a moment—"Ah—and I see you've made it past your "Second Saturn Return."

Thomas was growing into the senex, the wise man archetype, as well as holding the persona of the wise old "Fool on the Hill." And I'm sure he knew it. I'm sure he loved being that crazy character: the old artsy guy who owns the bookstore on Chestnut Street.

I shot him a comforting look while trying to think of words to describe this Saturn transit that I knew was much more subtle, and difficult. He didn't look at me, but stared into his pipe smoke instead.

"So…this year it feels to me like something is stirring uneasily in you….a little slow revolution beginning to happen. Saturn makes changes by challenging us on our unfinished business. He doesn't make it easy on us."

"I certainly have felt different in a way that I haven't felt for years. And also open to being in relationship again. That's new."

"Well, let's talk a little about how this Pluto squaring your natal Venus might play out. It feels like you're being drawn again into the underworld to explore something within yourself that wants to come up and be made conscious." He didn't say anything, so I went on: "Venus-Pluto relationships arise from unconscious complexes and become compulsive. They move into the realm of the taboo…lover's triangles, incestuous feelings, dangerous or surprising love affairs. The stuff of novels."

Thomas let out a big sigh and put down his pipe. "And when is that happening?

"Well, it's happening now and for most of next year. Do you know what I'm talking about? Can you feel this at all?"

"No, not really." Something felt awkward. "I don't have any of that Venus high drama stuff happening... not that I know of." And then he actually winked at me. I didn't think people still did that any more. It felt more like a cover-up than an attempt to flirt. He went on: "I just have my Sunday afternoon friends... the philosophers! No high drama anywhere. And you... you're a new friend." Just then the phone rang again, and again I didn't answer it, but turned it off instead.

He stood up. "We could finish this up later, and you could take your call. Maybe it's important. I could come back later. Why don't you come by the bookstore, and we can talk more about this, and make our book exchange?"

"Well, we're far from finished, but yes, that would be fine—why not? It will give you time to think about your chart. And I'd love to see your shop."

"Do you know what I think? I don't know your chart or anything, but I'd like to give you a book, right now. I can tell you have the same sense of adventure she has..." He took a book from his bag, a book by Karen Blixen: "Out of Africa."

"You know what she says? She says the cure for anything is salt water: sweat, tears or the sea. I think we all could use a dose of that now and then. I don't know why I say that now, but something tells me there's something here for you...maybe I'm a little psychic at times, I don't know. But I sense something's shifting for you..."

Silence. I raised my eyebrows, what did he know? "That's fine, Thomas, I look forward to reading the book, and seeing you again soon."

But it wasn't going to be the way I imagined, in fact, nothing was going to be the way I imagined, except that Thomas was right: the sea, my sweat, and my tears would wash over me and change everything. Could he know that?

When he left I picked up my phone messages. It felt as if I were indeed being thrown into the sea. This was the beginning of the Saturn Return.

Chapter 7
"Simple Grace"

"If we could read the secret history of our 'families' we would find within each person's life a sorrow and a suffering enough to disarm all hostility." Henry Wadsworth Longfellow

I picked up the messages on the answering machine. It was the nursing home—they called to say my mother had another stroke. I thought I was prepared psychologically for this, but one never really is prepared for the shock of such news; for the shock of possible death. But the astrology charts were blatant in their verdict. All the signs were there: the subtle and foreboding omens of a mind and body slipping away.

I feel exhausted in dealing with a problem that has only one solution—death. This is the final act in a long and tortured relationship that has been bandaged, but not healed. But no matter how much I may know that the end is near, and try to put it all in perspective, the reality is always a shock. And I can feel my grief...

This morning when I went to the nursing home, my mother was scared and wanted to talk about dying. I told her how I had heard that dying is sometimes compared to slipping out of an old shoe that was too tight. I rubbed and massaged her feet gently while we talked, or rather, while I talked—she seemed to like that. Then I stroked her hands for a few moments before I left and went back to my "sanctuary." It was hard to leave, but yet I couldn't seem to stay any longer, the truth was, I was scared.

The next morning I was back at the nursing home by 8:00 am. The prediction was coming true…or at least I thought it was. Astrologers proclaim that it is completely unethical to predict death, and the idea of "desiring death" for another is unacceptable for everyone. Yet during the past few months I had clearly seen the astrological "significators" for death in my Mother's chart, particularly as it was reflected in my chart. Death is more easily seen and predicted by looking at the chart of a person who is the closest to the one who may die. We were having Saturn Returns, and Jupiter, the planet of release is often implicated in death, especially in a case like this where I was the caregiver. Her Jupiter and my Moon were conjoined.

These were the thoughts that were swirling in my head as I walked across the cold parking lot to the nursing home yet again. I had been coming here every morning and I knew I had to face this adversary, this death, now. And I wanted to do it with patience and dignity, knowing that this moment in time was auspicious as well as ominous. It held hope for healing and the chance for love. But I could barely hold my courage any longer, and so I hoped the prediction of release would soon be coming true.

I dug my hands deep into the pea-coat jacket, and retrieved the fragment of paper that I had scribbled on months ago—it was that quote from Henry Wadsworth Longfellow that had been sustaining me through the last few years of Mother's illness. I stopped and read it again: "If we could read the secret history of our enemies we would find in each person's life a sorrow and a suffering enough to disarm all hostility." I had changed the word "enemies" in that quote to "families." It certainly resonated with me now.

The air smelled warm and chemically sweet in the nursing home. I entered the elevator alone and was inched along to the fourth floor. The door opened and as I walked across the dining room I looked for Mother. She wasn't there. The other patients were eating, though many had their heads drooped over as if they were asleep. Hardly anyone talked. The lights on the Christmas tree twinkled in the somnolent dreamscape.

As I walked down the quiet hall I could feel fear rising like sap in my veins, and it began pouring out my hands. The limbs of my body felt weak. The door to her room was open but I could see the curtains drawn around the bed. Could she have died during the night?

Pulling the curtain open I saw her eyes were closed, her mouth was open and the breathing labored.

I sat down next to her and took her hand in mind and began praying to God to release this Soul.

"Isabelle?" she said, as she stirred and opened her eyes. "You've come." Her voice wasn't more than a whisper.

"Yes, Mom, it's me." I leaned closer. Our eyes locked into an embrace. It was as if she was holding onto me, to life, by the very force of our gaze. We stayed that way a moment, then I had to look away, to let go.

"I'm scared…lonely. And I don't think they like me here. The nurses don't like me."

"No, that's not true. And, of course you're feeling scared and alone. Such a hard time you're going through… but you're safe, Mom, really. It will all be Okay." My words sounded unconvincing, like weak medicine that would do no good.

I understood about her loneliness, this particular loneliness, but I could barely hold myself together now. There was no one here to help me "hold it" now; no one I could go to. But I shouldn't have had to be the one to hold her loneliness when I was younger—it seemed to permeate me at times because I cared and believed I could "fix it" for her. And I tried for so many years. I couldn't help but think how loneliness is a bit like an infectious disease, and I didn't want to catch it or send it on. Yet I wanted to be there for her; to reassure and comfort. A delicate balance.

I could hear the heavy footsteps of someone approaching. The nurses asked if I would wait outside as they checked her vital signs. Vital signs...that meant something different in my astrological language. Mother was a Capricorn, a German Capricorn. A cardinal sign that was very vital.

I walked back towards the dining room and collapsed into a chair. Staring blankly across the room I let my eyes linger on a simple crèche of Mary and Jesus in the stable. The naïve tackiness of the plastic figurines didn't strike me as cheap or trivial this time; instead I remember how Mother had devoted so much time each year to creating a good Christmas for my father and I. Every year she would set up a Victorian Christmas village underneath the tree—an idyllic village scene where there was always pristine snow, where the skaters always had a glistening mirror lake, and the warm lights of the Catholic Church were always welcoming. She had been a good mother.

But some would say she had not been a good mother. I could still hear my mother's voice rattling around my psyche—old tapes that never seem to leave: "Isabelle, you must do this! If you cannot do this for me, I tell you I will die. I will kill myself, and your uncle knows this. He will tell others why I died—because of you." This was how I was raised—-there was no freedom: "Do this, or I will commit suicide and others will know why I died. You must do what I say." How much pain and fear she must have held within, to threaten that to her only child.

In time we had each forgiven the other, but now we needed something beyond forgiveness. The time for miracles was past, but could we hope for something more now—some simple grace? I thought of the simple grace I had felt on the day of my first communion. Dressed in white, like the little bride of Jesus, I wondered if I would feel a tingling as the wafer, the body of Jesus, was placed in my mouth. I believed in this little miracle, and so I experienced something, even if I didn't shiver with delight—I could feel the sacredness of the moment.

As I grew older I lost the peace that came with such simplicity and embodied faith, but in its place came a trust in the cycles of life and nature, leading again to a comforting cosmology of meaningfulness. Astrology had given me that—but now—what would happen if the astrological signs that predicted my mother's passing at this time didn't happen? Would I lose my faith? Would I lose faith in the synchronicity and correspondence that existed between the astrological chart and timely unfolding of events? Would I lose faith in God?

I was too tired to think—too tired to attempt to read the mind of God—too tired to think of the relationship between God's mind and the Soul's will. The charts seemed to reflect what was happening now, but all I could do was to let my head fall onto the table in in front of me like the other residents of the home. Maybe this is what's it's like to die here.

For the first time a slow cleansing trickle of tears began to fall as I allowed my thoughts to drift back to my study, to my sanctuary room. I sat there staring at the astrology charts—dreaming—watching how the signs had changed once more, but like in a bad dream, I was unable to see clearly, to answer questions...I couldn't remember what the signs or symbols meant nor if it was an ending or a beginning, or even whose it was.

I awoke to the soft touch of a nurse's hand on my shoulder. "You can go in now, dear."

Sitting down next to the bed again, I took Mom's cool hand in mine. I could see a slice of untouched mashed potato on her table, and gingerly I placed a small forkful of it in front of her lips. She opened her mouth and took a small bite and I could see the barest hint of a smile. She looked so very old, and yet seemed so very young; like a sick child who couldn't feed herself. I wanted to feed and comfort her. I hoped I had been doing that, but when is it ever enough?

"Thanks honey...I love you..." I took both her hands and held them, trying to infuse them with warmth and life. Then I waited for the "BUT..."—for the rest of the sentence to unfold—the part where she would tell me what she needed next and why. But it didn't come. There wasn't any more she chose to say this day. I was shocked.

"I love you too..." I said, surprising myself as a warm blush came over me. Maybe this is what "healing" feels like. Then she closed her eyes as if to close our session as she drifted back to where she had been. I was shocked and touched. The "I love you" wasn't followed by anything else. We both just let it sink in. Then I waited and waited. She was fast asleep.

I got up and walked back to the elevator, and pressed "Down." I couldn't wait for the slow elevator to come to the 4th floor. My courage was tenuous, almost leaking away. Again the paradox—the fear of death, and the shock of feeling loved. The healing of some old wound was almost more than I could take. I couldn't stand still—I spotted the "Exit" sign and ran down the steps into the fresh cold air outside. It now filled me with life.

Early the next morning the doctor called me as I sat at my computer. Mom had just died. I looked over at the cool blue light of the computer screen and saw that Jupiter, the planet of release and relief, had just conjuncted my Sun, and was aspecting Mom's chart as well. We had both been blessed.

I stared blankly at the signs and the synchronicity of "endings and new beginnings"—those euphemistic terms that were splayed all over the charts, but still a wave of sadness enveloped me as I remembered the painful ambivalence of our love. But it was finished now, and the ending had been both predictable and not predictable.

I turned off the computer screen as a ray of golden morning light shot through the window and warmed my face. I was in awe of the love that had appeared, and finally let myself inhale the hope of a new day. I stood up and moved to the window letting myself be bathed in sunlight and gratefulness for the small miracle of our last visit—we had indeed been blessed by simple grace.

Chapter 8

"The Devil is in the details..."

"It's fine for you not to come," I said, trying to control the tone of my voice. "Peter, I get it! You're 3000 miles away at your conference and you don't need to come. It's a lot of money and time you don't need to spend, and I've already handled it. I just wish you would...keep in touch."

"I'll come if you want." Peter's voice was sincere and I believed him.

"The funeral will just be me and a few of her old friends." I twirled the old phone cord tighter and tighter around my finger. "Fine...fine...." I kept saying. "But where is Sophie? She hasn't answered my emails or her phone."

"Really?" Peter was surprised. And then it all stopped being "fine." Peter assumed I was in constant contact with her. I wasn't. I assumed he was in contact with her, but he wasn't. He hadn't talked to her in almost a month.

"Last time I talked to her she was so impatient with me—she said she'd call me back in time, not to worry, etc etc.etc. I figured she was upset and would call me any day. I guess I didn't listen to those "etceteras" as closely as I should have! But you, Peter, I thought you were really tight with her now!"

"No! Why did you assume that?" His tone was beginning to sound really snappish. "Maybe Sophie was taking some time off from both of us so she could get over this situation, this separation. Maybe she needs to feel more independent."

"Now you're assuming!" I snapped back. "Will you try to get in touch with her? I will too…it's going to be fine." I said. "Just keep in touch." And then we hung up, both of us feeling that it wasn't fine.

The funeral was the next day, and it was as fine as it could be. I talked to a few of Mother's old friends, and a few of mine. It was sad, but our 'healing words' the night before she died had changed everything for me. The funeral wasn't important; our healing was. It felt as if we had done our work together, and there was a warm glow in my heart now that wasn't there before. We were both at peace; I could say I loved her.

❧

The funeral was barely over; I was back in my study when the phone started ringing the moment I walked in. A woman from a British hospital somewhere in "Lindisfarne" on the northern coast of England was on the other end of the line. What? It wasn't making sense. She said she was calling to tell me that Sophie was in the hospital there.

I wasn't really hearing or thinking. I was dreaming. In the dream she told me that Sophie had almost drowned. The voice on the other end of the line said my daughter was barely conscious by the time someone found her and pulled her out of the ocean—she had fallen amid the fast tides that inundate the island's waters, and apparently she had a concussion and a fractured arm.

The woman said they were trying to call her father—she said Sophie was stable but seemed exhausted and depressed, and that we should both come now.

I remember writing down all the needed information. I remember calling Peter right then and making flight arrangements to leave tomorrow, together. He'd take a night flight from California and meet me at the airport in Boston. I seem to remember him saying that the last time he'd talked with Sophie she had said something about "maybe going on a pilgrimage" to a sacred island with a name like that, with her new Christian friends. But Peter thought she was just thinking about it…and of course, he said, I had enough to worry about with the funeral, so why bring up just another one of Sophie's schemes and dreams?

I didn't want to remember more. I needed to pack my bags and meet him at the airport tomorrow—and fly together to Sophie's bedside.

I began coming back to this reality. I walked in circles around the room, then sat down and opened the computer.

OK, I thought…. Sophie had gone on "pilgrimage" to this holy island of Lindisfarne—a dream which she'd never told me anything about. She had an accident. OK.

I pulled up her chart—Sophie had transiting Uranus squaring her Sun, Mercury and Mars. There was Uranus, the unpredictable and accident prone one joining up with Mercury, the 'god' of travel and miscommunication with Mars, the 'god' of adventure and war. I didn't care if the symbolism was "right on" she still could have played it out differently....was this Uranian "recklessness"? Astrology be damned! It doesn't matter what the aspects are—it doesn't help.

How could she keep all this from me? How could she ignore me? This wasn't like her. But now it was like her. I looked at the last email she sent me weeks ago. It sounded so kind—she sounded happy, she sounded like a different person. She had fooled me. She signed it "I love you always." I printed it, and reread it.

There was nothing in it about this—nothing about Christianity—nothing! Nothing! I squeezed the paper in my hand and threw it on the floor. Shit! Bullshit! She wasn't telling me what was going on. She told Peter more—didn't he say she had plans to walk 'through the waters' with the other "pilgrims"? Didn't she know about the undertows of incredibly fast tides? She must have left the group at some point—was she depressed? Manic? Suicidal or enraptured? I'd always hoped that Sophie and I could take a trip to visit the sacred sites of Europe together, but instead it had come to this.

Calm down, I kept telling myself. I decided to "google" this holy island of Lindisfarne to figure out what drew her there. It said that this was where the "lantern of Celtic Christianity was first lit." Grrr...And it went on: "A curious sense of timelessness, of being in time but not entirely of it, pervades this place where the veils between the worlds are thinner...the rhythms of the tides insulate the island twice a day, and these govern all." I kept reading, astonished at how many "pilgrims" died over the years trying to walk across the waters to the island this way. People like her who don't swim well, and get caught in the insidious undertows.

Was she risking it all for God? Sophie is a very determined Scorpio. I respect her privacy, and I would always trust that her "interest" in Christianity wasn't cultish. However she had no obligation to tell her me her plans.

I closed the laptop, and tucked my journal in the bag with it. As I packed, all I could feel was shame that I didn't know. On the phone Peter said he knew Sophie was leaning towards Christian fundamentalism; didn't I? I didn't remember any of that. Sophie, the 'only daughter of an astrologer'—ah—what must she think of me?

I couldn't calm down. So I brought up the internet again and started reading more; maybe I could understand this somehow. Apparently the isle of Iona, up farther off the Scottish coast was the center of Celtic Christianity, and spawned many of the other monasteries like Lindisfarne and Whitby. They were spiritual centers, yet also epicenters of power struggles between the Celtic Christians and the Roman Christians.

I knew Whitby. Peter and I had actually gone there as part of our honeymoon. We were enchanted by the monastery on the ocean and its strange history. It was at Whitby that the largest clash occurred between the Roman Catholics and the Celtic Christians. The Romans won. It was supposedly where the great debate on the exact date Easter would be argued, and when the Romans patriarchs overpowered them and it changed a lot more that the date of Easter....the monastery there was led by a woman, St. Hilda.

Well, that was all very interesting, but felt irrelevant now. Sophie's spiritual journey was a lot more important than I realized, if that's what this was all about. Maybe she was trying to find her way between Peter's more Buddhist ways, and my more pagan-astrological ways. The Celtic approach to Christianity held more mysticism than either of our approaches, and perhaps she saw it as her way. But then she fell....

I dragged myself upstairs to bed, and tried to imagine seeing Peter again....and meeting him this way. There was no more time to write or think or even feel. I doubted I could sleep. And then I remembered Theo.

I immediately called up Thomas and he agreed to care for him while I was away...in fact he said, he would pick him up for me right then, as he was out for a walk at the moment and nearby. I decided to forget about sleeping—I needed to pack and be ready to leave by seven in the morning. Thomas offered me a ride to the airport....thank God for Thomas.

Chapter 9

"Love is an act of endless forgiveness, a tender look which becomes a habit. ~Peter Ustinov

"Hell is hot, isn't it?" I shouted to Peter while running to catch our plane at Boston's Logan airport. But I was thinking about more than temperature. A little sweat usually didn't kill anyone. But I thought of how hell happens in the "in-between times": the times when you don't know if you will make it or not—those times between the biopsy and the result, between the labor and the birth, between the knowing whether you live or die, are loved or not.

So here we are in the "in-between knowing" if Sophie would live or not. I was probably imagining it worse than it was, and maybe, despite our mutual reluctance, this might just be a good chance for Peter and I to talk after this time of silence, who knows? Maybe we could bridge some in-betweens together.

I glanced again at our tickets as we walked down the aisle: "Isabelle Cocroft: seat 15 E Peter Cocroft 15 F." He had the window seat, I had the aisle. We were the last to board the plane with only 5 minutes before take-off. Thank God the air-conditioning would be on soon.

I put my hand on Peter's arm. "You could have told me about what was happening with Sophie—Peter, you know that was wrong to keep it from me!" He looked away and said nothing. I was keeping my voice in the "rational range" trying to pretend I wasn't as hurt and angry as I felt. So he wasn't going to defend himself.

I pulled out my laptop and opened it to my chart for today. Transiting Mars opposing my Venus; Mercury squaring Uranus at this very hour. Hm…it didn't look the way I wanted it to look. As astrologers say, it's not "auspicious" for flying when Mercury, Uranus and Mars aren't in harmony. And I knew that Pluto, god of the underworld, was still squaring off to my Libra Sun—my basic identity. Sigh…not good aspects if one has a fear of flying. I closed the computer screen and rested my eyes as I listened to the engines struggling to turn over. The overhead light bleeped on and off.

Peter pulled out a book to read. I snuck a look at the title: "Truth is a Pathless Land; Krishnamurti." So he was still a philosopher at heart. But Peter had been deeply ingrained with a rationality that sometimes seemed to have no room for me, or my work.

I pulled out my journal, and read an old entry I had written—a quote by Francis Bacon: "A little of science estranges a person from God, a lot of science brings them back to God." In my mind, believing in God, believing in astrology, and believing in love were all related. My God wasn't Sophie's God, or Peter's God, and somehow I knew if things were going to change, I was going to need to learn to let our differences be okay. A deeper tolerance and love was calling....

But....I wasn't going to dwell on that now, or our differences. I closed my eyes and waited. It was 15 minutes past take off time and I listened to hear the reassuring sound of the engines starting up. Could they have overheated on the tarmac?

I caught the steward passing by. "Is there any chance of getting the air turned on?" I asked, in my most pleasant, but transparent voice. Why was it so hot in here?

"I'm sure as soon as soon as the captain can do it, he will." If the steward was a dog, he would have bitten me, or at least snapped.

Peter waved his hand as if to quiet me, to get me to calm down. He closed his book and his eyes. I tried not to see that as being dismissive, knowing that Peter was not always aware of how he affected others. He meant no harm. I stared at the curling wisps of hair on his forehead and saw again that face with the same serene kind look I had always loved.

And then I looked away—what would he have thought if he saw me staring at him now—a woman with sweat running down her face in rivulets, smearing her eye make-up into dark raccoon eyes. I wondered if he could still see the wide eyed yearning in my eyes, the woman he had once married. But he didn't look. The eyes of this post-menopausal woman were the same, though the blonde hair was now short and cropped rather than long and loose.

I looked instead at my hands and stared at the finger where my wedding band had been. I had left the finger bare, but had bought myself an onyx ring for the other hand; a ring that recognized my new commitment to myself. I was trying to take good care of myself these days.

I looked down at my computer, and put it under the seat. Even it was making me hot. I wiped the sweat off my forehead, and squeezed my hands together.

Peter's eyes remained closed. It was a bit annoying, really—he could at least ask me how I was feeling. "So Peter," I finally whispered, "What do you think? I mean, is this plane going to take off?" I wanted to say more, but this was at least a start. He opened his eyes as if he was coming out of a deep trance. I couldn't help but think how people with a lot of Neptune-Pisces energy in their birth chart seem to be able to block out this world. He looked like he had retreated to another planet, but I was not going to sit here alone in silence. I nudged him.

"What?" he asked. He knew I was disturbing his attempt to escape and that I did it anyway. The attendant interrupted us: "We're being delayed—the captain has suggested we offer you complimentary snacks or beverages, as we may be stalled for a while longer."

"For how long?" I asked.

"Oh, not long, I'm sure." The attendant smiled, shrugged and lifted his eyebrows wickedly. I guessed he was gay, and wondered how he felt seeing people like me squirm. Some gay men are so nurturing, and yet some seem to have such a wounded attitude towards women. I shouldn't make sweeping judgments like that, as I hate people making judgments of me as a woman or an astrologer.

"I'll have a white wine with ice, and what about you Peter?" He shook his head no, and pulled out an eye pillow and put it across his eyes.

I touched Peter's arm again. "Peter....Do you have to close down? I know you and Sophie are trying to have independent lives, and...." He nodded his head yes, but said nothing. He didn't take off his eye covering. "You know," I continued, "we're going to be spending a lot of time together."

He sighed. His hand reached over for mine and tapped mine as if to calm me down. Then he refolded his hands on his lap. How condescending I thought. Damn him! He had no rings on his hands but they were more wrinkled than I remembered.

I sipped my wine. We were now seriously delayed. I could feel the mood in the cabin and it wasn't good. People began talking more, but not us. Another ten minutes passed. I finished my wine. Peter's forehead was dripping with sweat.

"Peter?"

"What? What do you need?"

"I don't know.... to talk?" I paused. It was hard to make small talk in hell. "What are you thinking?

Why didn't you tell me what Sophie was doing? What's happening to us?"

"I don't know Isabelle. What does it say there in the chart?

I gritted my jaw. "About Sophie? About us? About this plane? I thought you didn't believe in astrology, so why are you asking me about it now? Is that sarcasm or do you really want to know?" I tried to take a deep breath. "I'll tell you—things don't look so good right now."

He didn't say anything. Perhaps he was pondering the questions. "I know, Isabelle, I know…." The engines started up again and then stalled with an irritating whine. Their noise made it impossible to talk quietly. I covered my ears, but could still feel panic rising.

Then I almost yelled at him: "Do you still believe in us? I mean, despite all the rational reasons to the contrary, do you still believe—?" I was drowned out.

The engines let out a terrible noise. Peter grabbed my hand. "In what?! he asked. He looked terrified. He was barely breathing, and I could see the sweat pooling on his face.

Then he took me off guard and brought my hand up to his cheek and moved my fingers across his lips. What? Why was he doing this? Did he think we were dying?

Leaning over towards me he looked at me as if for the first time. His other hand reached for mine. "My god, Isabelle….you know, there aren't any atheists in foxholes. At moments like this, we all believe. And I do believe in you...in us. I always have."

He held my hand against his cheek. Sometimes Peter wasn't good with words but that tender look softened my heart and a little stream of forgiveness started seeping in. An old song played and replayed in my head: "The Water is Wide...I cannot cross over..." Was this about the ocean we were trying to cross now or the waters Sophie failed to cross?

But it wasn't Peter's voice or the song I heard just then—instead it was the intercom: "Please leave the airplane immediately; do not bother to take your overhead luggage. We will get it to you. Exit immediately to the front of the plane. Attendants will be here; do not delay; when you are de-planed we will reroute each of you to other planes that will take you to your final destination point."

Nobody panicked, but to say we walked out quickly was too mild. I overheard a steward talking to another steward about a small "fire" and how it must have blown out an engine. Or at least that's what I thought I heard, over the din of confused passengers complaining loudly.

We all moved in a hot steaming noisy roll off the plane, and Peter was quickly shuffled off to one small plane and me to another. Peter Cocroft and Isabelle Cocroft were each going on this journey separately. Why had they separated us on the smaller planes? There were no rational answers. Everyone seemed to be in a rush, and apologizing but giving no answers.

As Peter and I started saying good-by, his eyes lingered a second longer than usual on mine. I just stood there, and then he kissed me. Nothing dramatic, just a quick statement. I remembered the words: "Love is an act of endless forgiveness" but I could feel nothing.

In the coolness of the second plane I began returning to myself. I remembered thinking how the French philosopher, Sartre, once said "Hell is other people." We were not in hell, and yet—nothing had really changed except a minor intimidation of death and—instead of hell, I felt a touch of something like hope as I sat on the last flight, alone.

Chapter 10

"If you don't get lost, there's the chance you may never be found." Paul MacNeil

Peter and I walked into the hospital room together. I was scared. Peter was quiet. The nurse was just leaving. "Just a few moments for this first visit," she said sternly. We nodded our heads.

Sophie looked sleepy but managed a little smile. "Wow, well, this is nice, I guess. I mean you didn't have to come here." We hugged her and I fought back tears.

"Are you OK? What did the doctor say? A concussion?" I said, pushing back the tears. I couldn't imagine not being here for her, yet so much had been left unsaid for too long.

"Yes, but they said I'll be out of here in a few days." That was hard to imagine. She looked pale, thin, and had blue-ish circles under her eyes. She slid her hand through her thick auburn hair; that hair that made her look like a pre-Raphaelite's artist model.

"So Mom, my friend Kendra says you two are writing now. Astrology and all that. It must be nice for you."

"I'd rather have been writing to you." I replied. Guilt and accusations were seeping from my voice. I could feel how shaky and cold my hands were. I folded them in my lap, and waited. There was a long pause.

"Mom died." I finally said. "Did you know?" I knew she didn't know, so why did I say that?

Sophie's face softened. "No, I didn't. I'm sorry. Really. I wish I could have been there, for both of you." As her face relaxed my heart re-opened.

I lowered my head and looked down at my favorite chestnut-brown shoes. "I think it was her time to go…I tried to help…I told her that dying is like getting out of a pair of shoes that have become too tight." Looking up at Sophie, I gathered more courage—"But I don't understand, what happened?"

Sophie looked mildly annoyed. "It was my mistake. We made the walk out to the island just fine, but then I wanted to go see the other tiny island, St. Cuthbert's island—it was his retreat place. I went out there by myself one morning just as the sun was rising, and on the way I must have stepped in something, or slipped on something in the water, and fell. And then I swallowed a lot of water I guess. I don't remember more, except what they told me."

Peter nodded. "They told us how they found you. Sweetie, I wish you had told us you were coming here!"

"But now you're here." She added, smiling. "Maybe it's a good thing." Then she turned to me: "I've become a Christian, you know."

"I know. Is that a problem…?" I asked. She looked away. "Was this a pilgrimage with your friends from Providence?"

"…yes, but not with my boyfriend. We broke up. Like you guys broke up. No big deal, right?" She sighed.

"I never said that, Sophie." I said, shooting a glance at Peter who immediately stood up and walked over to the window. I wondered what he'd said to her about us.

"Lindisfarne is a sacred island, did you know that?" Sophie's face brightened. "See for yourself…take a walk out to the old castle, and visit the monastery ruins…there's something special happening there. The veil between the worlds is thinner here…."

Peter turned around and snapped back: "Thinner?! You're thinner! We'd rather have you stay with us in this world, Sophie, I don't need it any thinner and neither do you."

Sophie looked at me blankly, then covered her face with her hands. "Sorry, I don't believe we have as much choice in these things, as you two do…"

"There are so many layers of Truth, honey, we don't know what we're doing half the time!" My arms began waving. "I know you think I'm a professional "know-it-all" or something, but that's not how I see it. You can call it God's will, or just an accident—but I believe there are layers of God's will and *our will* that work together and have meaning, but…" I was suddenly at a loss for words.

"But, what?" Sophie burst in. "Truth is simple."

"I think it is too, we just don't see the whole picture, all the time. We're *human* Sophie, we all make mistakes, do unconscious things and..."

Just then the nurse walked back in and interrupted. "Today: a real short visit. But you can come back tomorrow," she said. I couldn't help but think she must have been in the military in her last life.

I wanted to stay with Sophie and I could see that Peter didn't want to leave either. Sophie's eyes looked glazed, sad, and she looked older than when I had last seen her only months ago. But we left as we were told, and we promised to explore the island like she told us to do before coming back tomorrow.

As Peter and I kissed her on the cheek I was already feeling that we were in some strange waking dream but I didn't like the thinness of the veils one bit.

And so we explored the island. The narrow winding road that led to the castle was cut into on one side by the curving line of the ocean. On the other side was a long rolling field with sheep happily lingering and cows that curiously seemed to be nodding their heads at us. Butterflies and tiny birds flew about our heads fearlessly.

As we started our walk, Peter pointed to a sign with an arrow: "The Castle: 1 mile." The air was brisk, cool and windy, the skies moving, open, and moody with thick dark clouds. Every once in a while the sun would shoot through the clouds, piercing our numbness, flooding us with streams of light. I could imagine why most of the 150 inhabitants of the island believed in God. The beauty permeated every cell of my being.

We walked most all the way without talking. It did feel sacred, and natural. We followed the gentle curving path to the castle in the distance and walked along the road with others who had come there too…there was an older couple walking their sheep dogs, a young family with a baby, and a few individual 'pilgrims' who seemed to be like us—trusting that there was a good reason to be here. Peter would occasionally point to the horizon line where the endless sky met the blue gray waters and then sweep his hand over the whole vista, and sigh.

I was quiet. Something was happening within me that I couldn't find words for—maybe it was a little whiff of hope or maybe it was true that on this holy island the dividing line between worlds—between the living and the dead, between now and then, between heaven and earth—was thinner and the beauty made it all somehow good. Suddenly it was as if all my pores and synapses were opening up. I didn't feel sad or mad or guilty anymore, just a feeling of being one with it all; the beauty and the poignancy permeated me right to the core.

As we walked, Peter's hand brushed against mine a few times. It felt like an invitation, and I took it. Our fingers interlaced, and our feet walked in rhythm. By the time we got to the castle they were just closing for the afternoon, so walked out to the castle garden instead, sat down, and watched the evening sky changing colors over the silhouette of castle.

"This place is amazing." I whispered to Peter. "The curving road to the castle, the three of us being together again—it's all so unreal."

"The castle is just a museum, someone's home once upon a time." Peter said. "One of the few castles that were never actually used to defend or protect. It's a symbol, I think."

He was right; he was seeing symbolically. And though we weren't "home" it still felt like a good sign—we were circling the center, and perhaps we would all come back home when we were ready.

Chapter 11

"We are constantly invited to be who we really are." Thoreau

We arrived back at the hospital around two the next afternoon, after the tides allowed people to get off of Lindisfarne and over to "Berwick on-Tweed" where Sophie was—how frustrating to have to wait for the tides—how can people live like this I thought? But then as we walked around the little village, I began to feel again the mystique of the place and think that maybe we were the ones that were out of time with the natural rhythm of things.

Again it felt so awkward to be at the hospital. Suddenly a nurse rushed into the room: "Anyone for tea?" she sprightly asked us. We burst into laughter at this sweet intrusion of British civility. I swear the caffeine in the pot of Earl Gray tea felt like a small miracle.

And then it began. "So, why did you leave Dad?" Sophie turned to me with her usual quiet intensity. I wondered if she had considered this a good time of questioning. I didn't want to do this now. I didn't know where to begin, but Peter jumped in—

"Your Mom left me, Sophie, because we had grown apart. And we weren't there for each other at a few times when it really mattered." Peter looked at me as if I would supply the rest of the words then, but instead I just kept listening.

He leaned towards her: "Honey, I was simply exhausted at work, and your Mom was going through a hard time."

"So? That's pretty vague…" Sophie looked irritated.

I tried to jump to the rescue. "I was very upset… sometimes you just need to start over, and see who you really are, and who you're not—sometimes you have to reinvent yourself before you can go on. "

I could see Peter was going to help: "Before your Mom left, I didn't know what an anxiety attack was back then. I do now. I wasn't always helpful." I was surprised; I didn't think Peter ever had an anxiety attack. What else didn't I know?

I sighed. It felt as if our marriage was on trial, and I wanted to plead the fifth; to remain silent and not incriminate Peter or myself. Yet I wanted to hear how Peter understood it. I didn't want to make him guilty, nor did I want to offer excuses.

Silence.

Sophie looked at me expecting an answer, so I kept going: "I had been going to the doctor for mammograms that were coming back unclear; not good. It looked like I had cancer. And every morning mother would call on the phone—it was always all about her, about how her life was miserable, and how I could be doing more for her. We talked everyday till I was in tears. She believed I could somehow fix her life—for her. I tried but I couldn't."

"And the mood at home got tense. Dark." Peter knew he had to tell more of his truth. "It wore me down, and on some unconscious level I guess I decided not to be part of it all anymore. I couldn't hold it all together... so I "left" though I guess my body was still there. I left first, and then Isabelle...left one day. That's it." He took a deep breath.

Sophie sniffled. Maybe she had a cold too, or maybe it was an attitude. "I still don't get it. So Mom was crying about her mother, and having anxiety about cancer...so maybe she needed her shoulders massaged? Didn't you do that? I don't get it!"

I looked at Peter and wondered if he would say more. I didn't want to tell Sophie what was the last straw. There always is a last straw when it comes to ending relationships, but sometimes I think they're almost unconsciously orchestrated to prove a point. One look at Sophie and I could tell she wasn't satisfied with our answers, our story.

"And then one day I talked to the doctor and they arranged for me to have a type of mammogram that would let me know that day if I had cancer of not." My voice was very matter of fact. I hated to say it, but I had to: "And he didn't go with me." I added.

"Did you ask him to go with you, Mom?" Sophie looked annoyed.

"Yes."

Peter looked at me, then Sophie. His lips pulling back as if he didn't want to say more, but he did: "And I said, very simply, that I didn't want to be a part of your Mother's fear any longer, and I wasn't going to go with her." He looked sad.

I let out a long sigh and went on: "So that day I went to the hospital with a friend to find out if I had cancer or not. I found out I was dying—but not of cancer—of a broken heart. I had to leave to save my life. Maybe for Peter's life too."

"It's true." Peter whispered.

I wanted to soften this story because "truth" is so complicated and the stories we spin around things are often superficial and don't get to the heart of things. "Sophie, I felt as if I was losing my mind then. Stress can do weird things to your body chemistry. I wasn't there for your Dad too in many ways...we got lost together. We were caught in a web of fear and exhaustion, and "flight or fight" is usually what happens then. So I flew—away. To a place I had once been happy. To Boston."

Nobody said anything for a moment. Finally, I started chuckling:

"Okay...this is it: Sometimes life is like a box of crayons. Most people are like the 8-color boxes, but what we're all really looking for are the 64-color boxes with the sharpeners on the back. And we want somebody who will color things *our way*. We want them to color within the lines, and use the colors we want them to use."

I took a deep breath. How to explain this? "So there we were.... trying to paint the same picture, "color" the same life, and it wasn't looking pretty. I used to think of myself as a 64-color box of crayons—I thought I could blend, fix, and make it look good, all the time."

Peter grinned. "I bet you thought I had only eight colors—or even just black and white. That's because I wasn't sharing my crayons with you then—I hid them. I was too closed down to even know what I was feeling."

I wondered how Sophie felt about all this, and found myself stroking her blanket with my hands when I really wanted to stoke her and tell her everything would be just fine now. Instead I rambled on: "You know, I wanted life to be a warm rose color then. I was blue, yes a dark blue. I think Peter wanted "ocean blue" most of the time—or something like the blue of a Greek sky. Who doesn't? But at that time, I was like a kid muddying up my colors till they got really dark."

Sophie twitched. "Kids, coloring...I don't know. You were supposed to be parents, grown-ups. And—I'm not a kid anymore, you know!" She added petulantly. But she looked like a kid then. A little girl who sadly and desperately wanted her parents back and her life back. Her eyes started filling with tears and then overflowing.

Peter took her hand and handed her a tissue. I got up and sat on the edge of her bed. Just then, we heard the chimes of an old church bell through the open window, sounding out the hours, slowly...one, two, three...yes, it was three o'clock. And we were three. It was as if the Universe was echoing something about the natural order of things, and my body in response sent a shiver through me.

I looked out the window, spacing out for a moment. And then I heard it—someone was playing a guitar in the next room, trying to sing Judy Garland's version of "Somewhere Over the Rainbow." We all grinned at each other.

"Rainbows are symbolic, you know." Sophie smiled widely through the tears that were forming in her eyes. "You know they represent the covenant of new life for Christians." Peter and I both nodded our heads on queue like marionettes in an orchestrated play.

"It's a powerful symbol, for all people," I added, thinking that this simple moment of synchronicity might be a unique opportunity. "Can I tell you a story?" They looked surprised. "Just before my father died, I wanted to take him to this beautiful garden near where he lived, and I called him on the phone to ask him to go there—but he said, no, he just couldn't do it then. I was a disappointed of course, and the last thing I said to him was: 'You'll get there someday...even if it's over the rainbow.'

Now I don't know why that phrase popped into my head just then, but it did. And about a year before this I had asked him if he would send me a "sign" after he died to let me know if he made it safely to the other side. And he did." I took a deep breath.

Peter looked at me tenderly, giving me strength to go on: "When the call came the next day that he was actually dying, Peter and I jumped into the car and headed to their house. It was a perfectly bright sunny day. As we drove along the highway, suddenly I saw a rainbow in the sky. I couldn't believe it. And then I got it—there was my sign. I called home just then, and found out my father had died moments before."

Peter reached out his hand to me. And as our hands touched, Sophie reached out to us too as we drew ourselves into a circle, as if our lives depended on it. Sophie was encircled within us.

Thank God for gentle mercies. Thank God for little moments. The lump in my throat was too large for words.

Chapter 12

"Whatever you can do or dream you can, begin it. Boldness has genius, power and magic in it." Goethe

We returned the next day and continued "fumbling about" and talking as if all was normal and matter-of-fact. It seemed as if Sophie was becoming more and more pleased that we were both there. She had hated our separation, never understood it, and—for a moment I imagined this as a grand strategy to reunite us. Sophie was a bright, moody, and sometimes manipulative Scorpio—though I'd never say that to her.

Sophie convinced us that she was doing much better and that we should, in fact, both go out to explore more of the island since we had come so far. It made about as much sense as everything else, so we agreed again and left together, after more hugs and reassurances that all was well.

When we got back to the boat dock, to the place where we could have driven out to the island, we found that the tides had come in already and we had missed the chance to get there by car. The last boat had left. The tides had covered the road, and the currents were coming in fast. We were told we were going to have to wait till the next morning.

"Well," I said to Peter, "Shall we walk out into the water together and see what Sophie was trying to do? On her pilgrimage and all that? Maybe there is more to this than we understand.

So we began walking around the cold inlet with our pants rolled up, feeling the powerful surge of the waters rushing around our legs and the pebbly sands trying to bury our feet.

"What are you trying to do Isabelle? Relive her experience?" Peter asked. Suddenly he took hold of my hand—"Isabelle, I don't know what all this means, but it feels as if something larger than Sophie—larger than us—is orchestrating all this...I don't know, but I think our story isn't over yet."

"What story?" I asked, as if I didn't know what he was saying, but I needed to hear more.

"The story of our lives...you know, our life together."

He looked startled, as if surprised by his own words. I looked down at my bare legs in the cold water, and saw a hermit crab crawl over my big toe. I had no judgment of this sea creature, it wasn't good or bad, it was just was...fascinating; such innocence and such daring.

And then I looked at Peter standing there with his pants rolled up and his eyes as blue and earnest as I've ever seen them. I wondered if on some unspoken level we were each in the process of forgiving each other. And we just stood there for a moment, awkward in the silence.

"I don't know, Peter. I'd like to hope so." It was a bold move on his part to say that.

I'm shocked that we are daring to "feel together" again. I'm shocked that I'm smelling hope like a whiff of fresh sea air.

Reaching into the water I grabbed a handful of seaweed; it looked like a snarl of threads all tossed and wild. Yet, these were like the strands, the tangled threads of memory that hold a life together long after we've forgotten what was true and what was not true.

Peter steadied me, grasping my arm, as we tried to keep our balance in the rough currents. I kept thinking how we were here now, crossing these waters, but who knows when this moment in time would only be a whiff of memory remaining? How fragile our lives were.

Peter's hand moved down my arm and I could feel his calloused hand intertwining with mine. How could I ever sever the unfinished story of our life together? Could I release the old hurt and anger that had fueled my new life? What would happen now? Opposites were colliding in my psyche, like the tides rushing in and out at the same time, making me dizzy. I needed to get out of the water, if only for a moment.

Just then, someone started yelling at us and summoning us back to shore. So we walked back, hand in hand, and found that they had found a small boat still available to take us back to the 'holy isle.' The "water was wide" like in the old song, but, unlike the song, it appeared that we were going to cross over.

So now, I sit at this desk back at the "monastery" as Peter calls it, writing in this journal, trying to make sense of things. Peter is separate but near, in the room next to me. We are each in our own monk's cell, and all I can think of is the German philosopher's words on how "Boldness has genius, power and magic in it."

I wonder if I could be so bold as to begin again. Peter certainly had taken a bold step—his question of the rightness of our life together, of the continuing story of our life, was his statement of truth. I would need time to think about it, to feel into it. If I could only dream into this possibility and truly forgive, I might be able to be bold. But right now I'm exhausted. Boldness will simply have to wait.

Chapter 13

" I live my life in growing orbits...I am circling around God, around the ancient tower, and I have been circling for a thousand years, and I still don't know if I am a falcon, or a storm, or a great song."
~ Rilke

They let Sophie out of the hospital this morning, and she was back with us at the Retreat Center by late afternoon. I was working on my Saturn book when I heard a knock and then a voice whispering at the door.

"Mom....they're going to do a healing prayer circle for me—do you and Dad want to come?" Sophie asked.

I jumped up and let her in my room. "When?" I asked.

"Now...it's going to be downstairs in the chapel. Will you mention it to Dad? Where is he?"

"I don't know, but I'll find him. We'll be there." I gave her a big hug. I wished she had let us take her home from the hospital but she insisted that her best friend from the Christian community would take her back to the island. Not a big deal, she had said. I didn't know what was a big deal or not anymore, but I had the suspicion that this prayer circle was a big deal for her.

And it was. I rushed downstairs and found Peter in the library. We hurried down another flight of stairs to the little chapel in the basement and found Sophie already kneeling in the middle of a small group of young people.

They had formed a circle around her, and they motioned us in and we copied what they were doing—one hand was on her shoulder, and the other hand on our own hearts. Sophie looked radiant and the quiet sweetness in the room was palpable.

❧

But the silence unnerved me. A young man, who looked like the closest image to Jesus I'd ever seen, took out a tiny notebook and began reading: "Oh Lord, you who sit deep in our hearts, you who fill the sacred places and times with your numinous presence...You, the one who dwells at the line where ocean meets sky at sunrise and sunset...We ask you now to shine your golden light on your daughter, Sophie. We come here now to remember you, humbly asking for her healing, so that she may see herself clearly as being One with Thee, and One with all that is. We come together to hold Sophie in our hearts, and as we hold each other and ourselves, we dare to say: 'Thy will, not ours be done.'"

The Jesus look-alike shot a look directly at me. Was he wondering if I agreed?

He paused and then continued: "Lord, Sophie has come to you now for healing...cradle her in your arms, soothe her forehead with the warm wind of your presence. Remind her that she is always held lovingly in your hands, and that she will always be nurtured by your outflowing grace."

He paused again and asked: "Would anyone like to add to the prayer?" I looked at Peter, but his eyes were closed.

And then from somewhere deep inside me I heard myself saying aloud: "We all come again to you, Lord, as old and tired Souls still learning how to love...still learning that all people and events are our teachers... still learning that we each have within ourselves a deep reservoir of wisdom, love and connection. Lord, give us the courage to call on that inner wisdom....give us the chance to remember that we are all 'beloved' in all ways, at all times." I almost choked at the end of my whispered outburst.

I had no idea I would say that, or how or why the words just came. But they did, and "Jesus" gave me a little smile.

And so we just stood there with our arms curled around each other now, in silence. I could feel the electric energy of the group—and I must admit—the caring and connection at that moment seemed to unravel and un-do my old religious skepticism—even all my old ideas about "how religion always is and how it's always going to be." Maybe there were pockets of sweetness in the world, like this, that I had yet to discover.

After the gathering, Sophie hugged everyone and went upstairs for a nap. Peter and I walked around the grounds of the retreat house here and found in the garden, an inscription carved into a boulder. There was a triple Celtic Swirl on top, and then, carved beneath it into the stone, was this saying:

> *"I live my life in growing orbits, which move out over the things of the world, perhaps I can never achieve the last, but that will be my attempt. I am circling around God, around the ancient tower, and I have been circling for a thousand years, and I still don't know if I am a falcon, or a storm, or a great song."*
> *~ Rilke*

"Do you think that's the German writer, Rilke? It sounds more like John O'Donahue to me, do you know him, Peter—the Irish writer?"

"No. I guess I'm a bit 'parched' spiritually, eh?" He pursed his lips. "We're drinking up the goodness here, but Isabelle, don't get too enchanted here—this is the place that almost took Sophie's life.

"I'm trying to understand why she came here, and we won't get that, Peter if we can't get beyond our ideas of right and wrong, of what is true, and what is not.

Peter winced. "I can feel myself holding back—I have too many old ideas about Christianity. I'm trying to see what is good here now, not what they did wrong in the past....yet the past is everywhere, seeping out of the walls and rocks. And some of it is as quaint and sweet as this lichen and moss on this stone wall—and some of it—well, it will show itself, I think."

And it did. We walked around the gardens and ruins of the original monastery going back to the 7th century, to the remains of the monastery built by St. Aidan. We read the guide book about the history of the Celts here: how they were one of a "gentle people with a gentle way of life" with their natural built-in isolation from others. "Of course" said Peter. "This is also because they were protected by the menacing water that surrounds this island!

The guide book said that in the old days, if you dared to walk out or back from this island without knowing about the hours of the tides and the long distance, you might easily drown. In the 1950's, they added wooden towers/way-stations for pilgrims to cling to in case spiritual pilgrims, like Sophie, got caught midway. Later they added a small road connecting the island and mainland. But that frequently was not functioning and flooded by ocean waters.

How Sophie could get so hurt and caught up in the waters wasn't clear, but it sounded like she had wandered off from the group in to the even tinier and more isolated St. Cuthbert's island, just off shore.

And then it happened. We were standing outside an old stone chapel reading a plaque about the "one and only Way through Christ" when an over-zealous monk approached us. I walked away, but the monk was entreating Peter to understand something—all I could hear was Peter muttering something about how: "Truth is a pathless land." He kept saying it over and over, louder and louder, till the poor monk slunked away. This was a favorite saying of Peter's teacher, Krishnamurti—a man who didn't like any organized religion that purports to know "the way." Krishnamurti was an anti-guru, guru, who taught people how to be unconditionally free; or so he said. He had been raised by Theosophists to be the second coming of Christ but he had dramatically forsaken his role and promoted how to be 'free' from conditional thinking. He was a lot like the writer, Eckhart Tolle.

Peter was silent for a few moments after his exchange with the monk. Finally he let it all out: "And that is exactly why I can't stand Christians! They act as if they have a special foot-hold on God and it's their way, the Only Way, and—it's arrogant!" He was getting redder and redder in the face.

I squeezed his hand. "I don't want this tiff to spoil our good moments here and the beauty of this Celtic Island with all that...please, Peter." And so we continued walking till we found the pebbly cliff paths overlooking the English ocean. It took my breath away.

Then we began walking inland. The wind was picking up into quite a howl along the headlands, so we walked back into town and found a rustic Pub: "The Monk and the Merchant". The pub felt like a refuge from the storm, and it smelled of peat and old wooden beams. Men were sitting around the fireplace and several couples like us were lingering over glasses of red wine or dark ales. That was my first glass of wine. That's when he told me the news—

"Isabelle, I have to tell you something." He looked a little guilty. "I'm going to be leaving for Zurich, Switzerland tomorrow. I had signed up for a conference long before this happened with Sophie, and the dates just coincided. It's a special Krishnamurti gathering with Buddhists and others...."

"So where does that leave us?" I asked him, astonished by this unexpected news .

"It's up to you....I don't know. Would you and Sophie like to go meet me there after she re-coups?" He seemed nervous.

"I don't know." I was shocked. I took another long sip of wine. Did he have a lover that he was meeting there too? Or what…? My stomach churned. "Why would Sophie want to go there?

"And do you really want me there?" Some of my skepticism began returning. "Are you seeing someone else?" I boldly asked.

"No. You know I'm just friends with all those folks…you know how it is at Krishnamurti conferences." I'd heard that before. How was it really, I thought?

Suddenly he seemed pleased with himself. "I have an idea. Maybe you and Sophie could take a train down to the village of Whitby, first, and then fly to Zurich together. Do you remember our trip to Yorkshire when we were first married? Do you remember the monastery of Whitby? Those cliffs towering above the sea?" He waved his hand as if he were trying to sell me something. I didn't like where this conversation was going.

"Of course. What's the point?" I asked.

"It's another variation on this theme of Lindisfarne…but not so evangelical." He looked like he had just solved a mystery and all the parts would add up to a perfect completion.

Peter was right—Whitby could be a meeting ground for Sophie and me—where her evangelical Christianity and my "more pagan beliefs" might blend… .a mix of Celtic and pre-Christian spirituality. But still she had a job and friends, and why wasn't Peter making us a priority?

"Okay.…I could ask her." I don't know if I managed a smile or not.

I remember staring up at a Celtic Cross on the far wall—even in the dark pub—and thought how much it looked like one of Jung's mandalas. I tried for a moment to think like Peter; rationally. "So we could go from there to visit you in Zurich…and visit Carl Jung's home."

"Maybe.…but let's take it slow, Isabelle, let's see how it goes. I've committed myself to being at the conference for a couple of months. I'd planned to be in Zurich for a while—you know, before all this happened with us." Then he sat back in his chair, very contentedly, and looked around the room as if it was all set.

"Months?" I whispered, though I felt like screaming. "We can't—you mean, you don't think we need to be together now, you and I?" It wasn't even the time factor that was as shocking as his cool objectivity.

"No. I have to do this now, and when we're both back in the states we'll spend time together again. We'll have lots of time to date then."

"Date?" I asked incredulously.

"Yes, we'll date and see how it goes." He started squirming in his seat. And there was something else. I don't know what it was, but I felt it. I saw it in his eyes that kept straying from mine. He wanted us together, but he also wanted to be away. He wasn't committed to us as far as I could tell.

And so we quickly finished our glasses of wine, and all I could think of at that moment, was Thoreau's words: "We are constantly invited to be who we are." And who would I be now? An angry disappointed woman? Am I supposed to be grateful? Peter always says I have too high expectations. He's right.

ಹಿಣ

To: Kendra@gmail.com
Attachments: Saturn Returns and "Story of Sophie's Accident"

Dear Kendra~

I'm sorry our emails have been so few and far between! I'm attaching some pieces of my writing on the Saturn Returns. I get chances to write between visits to the mainland—I hope they will help you. Don't forget to look to what sign and house Saturn is in your chart as well, because then it will be more specific. Astrology is a synthesizing puzzle; but therein lies its magic as well! You must have the intuition to do it, and I sense that you do.

Ah...as for me, I am so much in need to have someone to talk to now, someone with your sensibilities...and yet I know we hardly know each other. I loved your encouraging response to my last email, and I will try to keep an open mind and heart on all things. You are such a wise young woman! You remind me of Sophie in some many ways, but you are twenty-nine and she's so much younger and with no apparent interest in astrology.

Anyway, you said in your last email that you love Celtic Christianity—but what is your spirituality really? I ask myself the same questions. Astrology and Jungian psychology are such a rich study and such a great mystery...but still....

what's at the heart of it? What's the link between the inner and the outer life? Does knowledge have a heart? I love how synchronicities arise in the reading of a chart—it's like the nuances of the Holy Spirit whispering insights, and the sacred geometry and language is so rich in mythology and history. But still...it doesn't warm the heart at night.

I wish I could get beyond my historical literal mind and really hold to what Jesus said about love and total inclusiveness, the way Sophie does. But it's hard for me to forget the history of the church and reach for the heart of God. I love how Sophie, with her yearning heart, finds such peace in Jesus. I even love how Peter finds peace in his more Buddhist-like spirituality, and I guess I'm living into an astrological symbolic life, finding meaning where I can. That's where I'm at now. A meaning-maker, but I'm struggling with it all here. The pieces just don't fall into place the way they should.

Today I thought of you, Kendra, when I found some on-line information on Saturn. It was about the medieval astrologer, Marsilio Fincino, was the first to express the "gift of Saturn." The gift—hah! From what you've said and how I feel, I think we're ready to return the gift.

Anyway, this medieval astrologer/astronomer, Marsilio, was apparently the first to recognize the good side of how Saturn can be the midwife of insight. He said that this is because Saturnian depression, or "melancholia" as he called it, creates a permeable boundary between consciousness and unconsciousness. This inner reflection, or depression, is experienced like a "falling into ourselves" that brings us to the point where we are no longer able to continue with life in the usual way...because we're not nourished any longer by what is happening in the moment. We're not happy with what the ego has achieved and what the world has given us, so we begin creating something new—he says: first insight, then action, then change. He says Saturn is all about taking the small steady steps, like the mountain goat patiently treading its way to the top of the mountain.

Sounds good, but at the moment I hate the feeling of "melancholia" I feel sometimes around Sophie, and I don't have insight into what she's thinking, so the feeling hangs in the air between us today like a gray mist. I'm holding back from trying to pull us out of this melancholia for the moment, but maybe in Whitby the gods will grace us...that is, if she comes!

Today I wrote more in the book...I said: "We often lose energy as we move through Saturn time passages, as we are often called to dance with an invisible partner. I certainly feel alone at times, despite whoever is around. They say the antidote to Saturn is Jupiter, the planet of expansion, grace and opportunities, and Venus, the planet of love and connection and beauty."

During Saturn Returns we are more permeable to feeling the defeats of the ego and often feel unseen and lacking in direction. Jung would say this space needs to be "held and allowed" until Saturn brings its gift of insight, creating a bridge for the Self to cross over to a truer destiny path. He talked about this in "holding the tension of the opposites" till the third way (the inspiration) is made clear.

So with Saturn Returns and Saturn transits—Jung says they can return us to peace and equilibrium—but during them it can be rough and lead to what he called "enantiodromia"—a complete and opposite change of attitude. This is when a condition is so extreme or severe that it polarizes into its opposite. I wonder if some of that is brewing for any of us or if we can simply hold the tension of the opposites, and wait till the third way appears.

I wonder what or who is the "reconciling third" for me that Jung wrote about? Writing this book is helping, but still I wonder who is my "invisible partner"? Is it my higher Self? She's invisible a good deal of the time, but sometimes I feel as if I almost get a glimpse of her.

When Sophie wakes up, we will decide if and when we are really going to get on that train and go to Whitby together...or not.

Sophie is often a late sleeper. Yesterday she explored the seaside by herself for a while as I retreated to my room to rest and read...yet even with my laptop and journal I feel this touch of melancholia—it's true, this is my Saturn Return, but I haven't seen the bridge to the future yet. I'm waiting.

So now I'm back at the retreat house and writing this letter to you....I wonder how you are and what you think of all this? Saturn delays things till the time is just right—do you think that's what this Saturn Return is now? And you? Send me news of you—and thanks for being there for me, for being my friend even in this crazy way of writing and connecting... you are there, aren't you? You're not just some figment of my imagination? Maybe you are my invisible third.

Fondly,

Isabelle

Chapter 14

"Whenever two or more are gathered in my name... there is love." Jesus

And so it happened, that Sophie and I went to the seaside village of Whitby. We checked into the hotel that sits right on the river that divides the Victorian side of town from the medieval side. On one side is where Bram Stocker wrote his novel "Dracula" and on the other side is the ancient monastery ruin where the future of the Christian Church was decided at the Synod of Whitby in 664 AD. Here is where the Celtic Christians lost out to the Roman Catholics. Here is where the monks and abbesses fought over such things as how to calculate the day of Easter celebration—here is where the astrological and pagan remnants of the church were finally squashed.

But Sophie knew I had a bit of an agenda by bringing her here, and she wasn't in a good mood about it. She knew I wanted to impress her with the fact that there was once a different kind of Christian Church other than the fundamentalist one she is connected with now—and—that there were women—like St. Hilda, who was the head abbess here, and who once had a powerful position in the church.

Sophie knew that I was hoping that the "supremely romantic ruins with panoramic ocean views" (that's how the brochure at our inn described it) would open her mind. I suspect she was steeling herself against it. But she agreed to come on this journey with me before going back home to her friends and job. This is our one chance to try to make things better. Peter went on to Zurich.

And so after we settled in, I suggested we walk up to the monastery as it was sunset and we still had enough light left. However, I'd forgotten how long a walk it is—and it's uphill. As we climbed the foot path via the "199 abbey steps" Sophie got cranky. She was still weak from her ordeal in Lindisfarne, and I began feeling guilty for encouraging her to do this pilgrimage with me.

"This isn't going to prove anything to me, you know…." Sophie fingered her cross chain and looked down as she continued: "I don't really care about history, I care about Jesus…and feeling connected with the Spirit." She stopped walking and just stood there. What I saw was a young girl who wasn't going to walk anymore, and a bit of smug stubbornness.

I lifted her head gently and looked directly into her eyes. "Me too," I said, "I care about Spirit and this is a sacred place too. It's a time for us—just us two. Do you remember Jesus saying: 'Whenever two or more are gathered in my name, there is love'?" She managed a little smile, and I motioned her to sit on the side of the steps in the grass.

We sat down and gradually her whole face softened as she looked out over the sea. "Okay, I'm here. Let's see what happens...but you can't force things, you know."

"True. But can I tell you something about the Holy Spirit? I asked. "Did you know, the 3rd person of the trinity was originally called *'Hagia Sophia'* which meant *feminine wisdom* in the original Greek? It was about intuition and feeling, and synchronistic touches of the Spirit. Her symbol is the white dove. But then it was changed by the Roman Catholics to the *Holy Ghost* at that first Council at Constantinople, and the feminine mysticism of it was suppressed...although we can still see it in the dove."

I looked out at a seagull flying over the ocean and thought that its outstretched wings against the sky looked like a sacred dove. "You know about the Dead Sea Scrolls? You know, when the lost gospels of the Essenes were found in those clay pots in the desert?"

"I know. I know about all that. Okay. So there are new gospels...but who knows what's really true? Mary Magdalene and all that. Perhaps they tried to repress the feminine side of God. But...that was the church, not Jesus! But—is that why you named me Sophie—Sophia?" She was frowning now and running her hand over the tiny blue wild flowers in the grass. At least she wasn't getting out of breath going up the steps.

"Yes. I love the sense of a feminine wisdom."

"And didn't I live up to it enough?"

"No, Sophie, you did! And I love you—always—no matter if you are evangelical or Buddhist! And I love that you've got such spiritual passion. Don't you think there's a middle-ground, a place where we can meet on all this?"

We were sitting on middle ground for a moment—not far from a towering stone Celtic cross. "That's what I believe in," she added a little sullenly, and pointed up to the cross.

"Me too…but do you see it Sophie? Look at that cross. It's different. There's a circle around that cross which changes its meaning. It focuses on the resurrection, the continuity of life, and…"

"Reincarnation…isn't that pagan?" Sophie got up and went over and stroked the green moss on the cross and then turned her back on me and looked out to the sea that surrounded us. A strong wind seemed to be gaining on us, turning the waves rough and the light was fractured by heavy clouds.

I stood up next to her and continued: "That's one way to look at that—but reincarnation was originally part of church doctrine, until the 2nd Council of Constantinople! Did you know that? And then the Roman Inquisition considered it a heresy, punishable by death—that's what they did to the Cathars in France. But the Christian Gnostics and the Essenes taught reincarnation, as well as this old theologian…Origen…. but it's not just about history, it's about—well maybe it's about not taking everything too literally…?" My voice began rising higher almost as if I was pleading with her, rather than retelling facts.

"You don't get it, do you? I don't care about *history*, I care about Jesus. What he stands for—why not Jesus, Mom? Why are you and Dad always arguing these things! I don't care about theories about God! I don't care! I want to feel it—here—"She banged her chest like a true pilgrim. "Have you ever experienced that—that warmth of God, in here? I don't think you have, Mom." She took a deep breath—"Come on let's get to the top of this hill."

We climbed the rest of the way up the cliff silently, watching the light breaking through the clouds onto the stone arches, lichen-covered tombstones and circled crosses. It was as if all of nature, all the stones, light, ocean, and wind were saying: "Talk all you want, but I am here."

So we stopped talking. The abbey was situated on a plateau, and behind it was a shallow pond. We circled around it slowly, and Sophie reached down to pick up something. The ruins of the cathedral and monastery were imbued with a deep silence. We didn't talk at first, then she broke the silence—

"This reminds me of Mayan ruins. Do you think our world will be in ruins soon—you know, after all those Mayan and astrological prophecies? Christian prophecy too."

"No, I don't. Some people joke about how the Mayans just ran out of room on the stone tablets, and that they got a good laugh at imagining people in the future seeing "the end" of the calendar, when it wasn't meant that way. But astrologers—we see it as a huge shift we're all undergoing with that square now between Uranus and Pluto."

We kept walking and looking up at the towering pillars and stony remains of the cathedral and monastery. It had once been a terrifying beauty. "Sophie, I see those predictions as the metaphoric death and rebirth from the age of Pisces to the age of Aquarius—and the tension of grand cross of the planets. We each have to bear the tension of the cross...don't we? We can circle that cross like a mandala, even if we don't know what's a metaphor and what's real death and rebirth."

"You mean you couldn't tell if I was going to die or not. Or if you're relationship with Dad will die or not. So you don't predict the apocalypse then?"

"No, I don't." I thought to myself, at least I didn't see an ending for mankind. For me, I wasn't so sure. I didn't want to tell her how the planets where aligning on my chart. That alignment was enough to make anyone shiver and draw up a final will and testament. Metaphor or reality, I didn't know if my phoenix-like experiences would be literal or not.

I could see the last of the visitors heading down the cliff-side as it was getting dark, and so we began retracing our steps breathing deeply of the salty-wet smell of the sea. The dappled light on the angel faced gravestones along the path seemed to make them come alive. It was luminous and numinous, I thought, or was it unnerving? Foreshadowing?

Then I looked down, and next to an angel gravestone was a heart. A perfect heart shaped stone. I picked it up and began rubbing it between my fingers. I once called these stones, "worry stones." What did it mean to find it just at this moment? Did it mean there was room in my heart for Celtic Christianity? Why not? I liked the rounding of the pre-Christian Cross. I liked the mandala-cross like look of a chart. It felt like a mandala, and if an astrology chart was about anything to me, it was about the peace of the mandala.

Sophie didn't see me pick up the stone. She had stopped and was gazing out to sea, and as I turned to look at her I could see a spark of sunlight reflecting off the ocean surface over her head. Nothing unusual really, but stunning nevertheless...wasn't that what happened at Pentecost? When Jesus returned after death to his disciples? Didn't it give them the gift of understanding and communicating in all "tongues?" Would Sophie and I ever be able to understand each other?

Seagulls circled around us. The clouds were thick and dark and it seemed to be getting colder. I didn't want to lose the possibility of our moment together. I searched my mind—"Sophie, do you remember the Irish poet, John O'Donohue? He talked about how the circle around these crosses is the circle of eternity. I closed my eyes and tried to remember his exact words. Then I whispered them to her: "The circle around the beams of the Cross rescues the loneliness where the two lines of pain intersect—the circle contains the mysterious nature of God's love…like the intersection of the outer world and the inner world."

"Pretty poetic stuff, Mom…" And then she slipped her hand through my arm as we walked, arm in arm with lowered heads, descending the steep steps again. A swift wind began whipping around our heads, and since we both had been wearing long shawls, pashminas, we covered our heads with them. I must admit I thought we looked a little "Biblical" descending the stairs, heads lowered, covered with humble shawls.

Suddenly a wild-looking young man—- a John-the-Baptist-type if I ever saw one—- came racing up the steps, muttering: "The Holy Spirit is not for sale…. not for Sale!" He stared at us as he hurried on by, and we burst out laughing. "You laugh. But they're selling cheap religious stuff down there, and it's wrong!" He pointed to the town and a shop at the very bottom of the hill. Then he stared at us, his face contorting and twisting—and then fell to his knees. "You two….you are blessed."

"Thank you, Sir…" Sophie put her hand on his shoulder. He stood up quickly, looked embarrassed for a moment, and then continued running up the steps.

Sophie turned to me with a sly grin, and then took out of her pocket a small black stone with a white line totally encircling it.

"Here, this is for you—and I didn't buy it! The circle, the line...is unbroken. A memory of this day," she put it in my hand. "And for you—for free! Maybe we really have been graced with...love." She laughed and looked down shyly.

I took her stone as if it was a great gift, imbued with magic, and I gave her the little heart shaped stone that I too had retrieved from the top of the hill—my "worry stone" that now seemed to hold more meaning; its heart shape a universal symbol. I enclosed my hands around hers with a little squeeze.

When we got to the bottom of the hill, we ducked into a little tea shop. There was a soft warm light permeating the rustic shop and I knew it was time to say good-by to Sophie and let her return to the States, to her friends and her life, and I would continue on to see Peter. Perhaps it was all unfolding as it should—it seemed as if we had taken the walk up the mountain and came down, different.

Chapter 15
"The Dutchman's Tale~"

So Sophie went back to the States, and I went on to Switzerland alone. Peter met me at the airport in Zurich right on schedule. As we walked into the city, the rain was pounding down unmercifully as we wandered through the streets of the old town looking for a place to stay. Finally, near exhaustion, we stopped at a café for a hit of caffeine—a cappuccino with a chocolate éclair hit the spot. Then I spotted a marionette shop across the street.

The rush of desire and adrenalin hit me more than the caffeine. I have a serious fascination with marionettes, especially with the ones that hold more life to them than what appears on the surface. I made a quick impassioned plea to go into the story-book- Tudor style shop. I knew Peter didn't usually like "to shop" yet he could see how excited I was getting and grinned at me.

"Why is it I love these marionettes so much?" I asked him. "Is it because I struggle with illusion vs. reality? Is it the hidden stories behind the hand-made puppets? Why do I love these "little people" so much?"

Peter looked perplexed and said nothing. I began spacing out—contemplating my own answer. Was it because I was an "only child" who was so often alone? Were puppets my special "friends" when no one else was there to play with? Was it because they seemed to hold a mystery innocence, and friendship all at the same time?

I asked him again to come with me—he nodded yes, and made the choice to be with me rather than sit on the "husband's bench" outside.

As soon as we entered, I gasped. Puppets and marionettes hung in every corner of the high ceiling room. In the back corner stood the shop owner over his worktable; a small wrinkled man with angular features and an upturned moustache that made him look as if he were from another era in Swiss history. He was lingering over his table, with wood shavings and doll heads and strings in disarray. He barely noticed us coming in.

An older woman was behind the counter—I assumed because of her age and round comfortableness, that she might be his wife. She wore an apron that looked to be from the fifties. Though she acknowledged us she seemed much more concerned with the music on the CD player.

And so, I became a child again looking for the lost Pinocchio, or whoever seemed to be tugging at my heart strings the most. Peter seemed to be getting quite amused with my enthusiasm.

"How about this one?" I yelled across the room to Peter. I held up one scruffy looking marionette of a street musician playing a fiddle. I had never seen anything like him before. He was made in Czechoslovakia and his face was weathered, his hair long and shaggy, and he had a look on his face I couldn't find words for...maybe a little sly, but tender, good-hearted. The price on his back didn't throw me into sticker shock, so I knew I wasn't going to leave there without him.

"He's...a little strange. How about this one?" Peter pointed to a sweet Pinocchio, but I already had a similar one that I had once "rescued" from the street market at London's Portobello Square. "Or this one?" He held up an even sweeter looking Cinderella. I shook my head no. I don't know why, but I don't like them when they're too sweet or too bizarre. My street musician was perfect.

"You look like the 'cat that swallowed the fish' Isabelle!" Peter stood there grinning at me. He looked at me as if I was twelve years old, then pointed to another puppet: "How about little Red Riding Hood here?" Peter was getting into it.

"But if I get that one" I said, "You'll have to get the one that is the big bad wolf—and then I'll have to run away from you!"

"You already have, my dear....did you forget? But my intentions were not like his....I was no wolf."

But Peter slipped his hand into the wolf puppet anyway and I slipped my hand into a red fox with a rather long delicate snout. He started nipping at me and I nipped back. We laughed.

"You beast!" I squealed.

"Me? You're worse! Look at you—this is what you do. Peck and nibble and bite. You don't understand I'm really a domesticated dog. No wolf."

"Really? You look fierce to me. And I'm just a shy girl fox…." I moved my puppet's hand coyly across her face. "I wouldn't hurt anyone. Especially you."

"I thought you didn't like me." The wolf replied.

"I thought you didn't like me." The fox replied.

"Maybe we just don't understand each other." I looked up at Peter. What I saw was a boy standing there. Not my husband or client, but a friend, and a young friend who wanted to play.

Re-inserting my hand into the fox, I nestled her snout into the wolf's ear and whispered: "Some foxes can't be trusted. But that's only when we're sad or desperate. But wolves are either wild loners or move with a pack… their tribe. Which one are you Peter? Are you a lone wolf?"

Peter looked like I had asked him a question of considerable importance. He thought about it a moment. Then his wolf nodded his head no, and I could see Peter's eyes looked teary. He turned away. Then he put down the wolf. I thought maybe he was upset with me, but instead he was looking for something else to play with. He grabbed a jester and began to talk in a strange voice: "I can make sad people smile. I can make you laugh. I can make you see things differently.

"Really?" I stood so close to Peter I could almost smell his apprehension. "Would you do that...could you make me see things differently?"

"I could." Peter turned to the shopkeeper who was now quite amused with our antics.

"We'll take the fox and the jester and...." He raised his eyebrows at me.

"...the fiddle player." I smiled so wide I felt like we had just played a scene in a Meg Ryan-Tom Hanks romantic comedy.

"Yes. I would like him...really." I picked up my little musician. "Maybe he could play for you—make you happy too?" I twirled and danced him around on the floor.

She turned up the music that had been playing in the background. I recognized the song—a sixties folk song called "The Dutchman." I was surprised to hear something so familiar and in English as well. It's a love song about an odd elderly couple, who still loved each other; despite their craziness. I had once known Steve Goodman who sang the song in a coffeehouse one year, lifetimes ago ; a young man who died before his time. It was written by Michael Peter Smith, still a popular well-loved musician. What bizarre synchronicity to hear this now...

"The Dutchman's not the kind of man who keeps his thumb jammed in the dam that holds his dreams in, but that's a secret only Margaret knows:" I whispered and sang along. I looked up at Peter who stood frozen like a mannequin. We stared out the window listening to the words:

When Amsterdam is golden in the summer,
Margaret brings him breakfast,
She believes him.
He thinks the tulips bloom beneath the snow.
He's mad as he can be, but Margaret only sees that sometimes,
Sometimes she sees her unborn children in his eyes.

"Do you believe in me Isabelle?" Peter asked.

"I don't know." I couldn't move. I was as scared as I was enchanted by the moment. Peter shuffled his feet as if we were about to kick something. "I mean do you think we could remember each other in that way, you know, when we get very old and can't remember anymore?" he whispered.

"You mean like them?" I pointed to the old couple. "I think we could."

He paused. "I think you know me like no one else will ever do." He took my hand. I could hear Peter humming along a little.

The Dutchman still wears wooden shoes,
His cap and coat are patched with the love
That Margaret sewed there.
Sometimes he thinks he's still in Rotterdam.
And he watches the tug-boats down canals

An' calls out to them when he thinks he knows the Captain.
Till Margaret comes
To take him home again
Through unforgiving streets that trip him, though she holds his arm,
Sometimes he thinks he's alone and he calls her name.

I looked down at our hands entwined together. It looked right. Familiar. "Maybe you are my Dutchman." I said. My words sounded as sentimental as the song lyrics.

The winters whirl the windmills 'round
She winds his muffler tighter
...they sit in the kitchen.
Some tea with whiskey keeps away the dew.
...he sees her for a moment, calls her name,
She makes the bed up...singing some old love song,
A song Margaret learned
When it was very new.
He hums a line or two, they sing together in the dark.
The Dutchman falls asleep and Margaret blows the candles out."

I could feel the tears starting to fill my eyes. Finally one large tear brimmed over the lid and I wiped it from my cheek. Peter saw that, and looked at me with soft eyes, then kissed me on the forehead, then the nose, then the lips. Something was changing. Something old that had been forgotten was being remembered, and it warmed me all over. I left the shop clutching "the little guys" and Peter's arm—maybe the cool rainy day wasn't going to matter so much after all.

Chapter 16
Entering Sacred Ground: Carl Jung's Stone Retreat

When you really know someone, you know what they like. And it should be simple to give others what they like, but it's not. We often don't even care enough to give ourselves what we need. But there are times when we do care and we do give.

This was one of those times. Peter cared. Or at least he cared enough. He knew what I wanted—he knew enough about me to know that if I was in Zurich there was only one thing I wanted—it was to see Carl Jung's stone tower on the shores of Lake Zurich. Jung, the famous Swiss psychologist, was my spiritual mentor, and for me, this was a chance to visit a sacred site.

I knew that Jung started building his private retreat late in life and that it took him forty years to complete. I knew that few people had ever seen his private retreat, and yet I had always yearned to see the dream images painted on the walls of his study and to see the sculpted images he carved on the stones surrounding the tower.

I'd seen photographs of him there in his eighties, pipe and book in hand, simply sitting and looking out over the waters. His sculpting tools and paints were sometimes shown in the background.

Jung's sanctuary was evocative of medieval times with its turrets, archways and courtyard. He built this "temenos"—this sacred retreat, as a place where he could study alchemy and astrology during his years of exile from the Swiss psychoanalytic community. It was here that he carved Greek, Latin and astrological hieroglyphics into massive stones. Here on the shores of the lake, was the "orphan stone"—an abandoned block of stone that workers had left behind—a stone that Jung carved for himself in recognition of his 75th birthday. Peter, as a clay worker, could understand Jung's comment: "I need not have written any books—it's all here on the stone."

And that was why we found ourselves outside the door in front of Carl Jung's house one day. The devastating news was that we couldn't go in. And what I had wanted to see was not even there! His mystical retreat was over in Bollingen on the Eastern shores of the lake, and not at Jung's family house in Zurich. So Peter took a photograph of me pretending to smile in front of the house we couldn't go into, and then we retreated in despair.

However—the next day Peter had an idea. And by late afternoon we were kayaking along the gentle shores of Lake Zurich gazing up at Jung's numinous stone tower.

"Shall we go ashore?" Peter asked.

I stared up at the imposing walls and the barred shuttered windows. This was not the kind of thing that Peter would usually suggest. He tended to be one who honored rules and regulations and was not one to trespass. This idea was so out of character for him; I must have looked at him as if he was crazy but I nodded my head.

"Of course," I said. "A little adventure." Peter knew me, and he cared. He wanted to do this for me.

And so we kayaked through the rocks and reeds along the shoreline till we hit ground. The ivy covered tower sat poised next to the lake. We could hear only the lapping of little waves on the shore and it appeared as if no one was in sight. There was a huge tree in front of us that looked like it had been struck by lightning. Could this be the same rumored tree that Jung had spent so many hours under—the one that had been struck by lightning the day he died?

We waded through the mud and held our breath as we approached the arched doorway of the tower. I could see the inscription Jung had carved over the door: "Vocutus Atque nonvocatus deus aderit". I whispered to Peter: "It says: 'Called or not called, God is present.'" I was certainly hoping no one else would be present but God. We could be in serious trouble for this.

"Come here," Peter motioned to me. He tried the latch on the door, but it didn't budge. Then, like a kid, Peter hoisted me up to look in through a window—an arched opening in the wall, and there was Philemon.

"He's there! Philemon!" I exclaimed. I could see Jung's painting of a wise old man on the curved walls of the study. He was huge, with the outstretched iridescent wings of the rare bird, the Kingfisher. Here was Jung's beloved muse, his spiritual mentor. I had just shown Peter a copy of this the day before in the recently released "Red Book." The book that was the journal Jung kept during those years of transition when he suffered the "divorce" from his mentor, Sigmund Freud. Some say, those were the years of his psychosis. For Jung, those were the years to paint, sculpt and play in the sand by the shores of the lake.

Peter lifted me down from the window. "Maybe we're pressing our luck…I mean our time." He looked at me as if he was hoping I'd had enough. We both knew there had to be some watchmen around here. I couldn't believe how quiet it was.

Peters face flushed. What did it take for him to disobey, to trespass, like this? This was not his style. But he was doing it for me.

We started to carefully make our way back, approaching the rocky shore. I kept staring at the carved stones around me—and then I saw it. It was a bird, large, recently dead, and with the same outstretched wings as Philemon. It lay under a carved image of a serpent in a rock, and it had the same dark iridescent wings. I reached for it, but Peter pulled me away and hurried me towards the boat.

The land began giving way to sand, then mud, and suddenly I lost my balance among the tall water weeds. I could see through the murky water that one foot had sunk deep between two rocks. My foot was sinking deeper into the mud, and the tall grasses looked like they could be a camouflage for snakes. I tried to pull myself up, but my foot was stuck. I yanked the foot out—and fell back into the water.

"Aggh…." I yelled, a quick sharp pain shooting around my ankle. "It's twisted!" I yelled again. And yet I could tell right away it was more than that. I wanted to dismiss the sensation and the after-feeling. It was as if I knew something, some little bone, had snapped; broken.

How can I say it? I just felt unhinged, a little broken. Shocked. There was a sense that my body wasn't going to let me dismiss this "fall" so easily.

Peter was next to me in an instant and what I saw reflected back in his face was a tiny terror—a sense that I was paralyzed perhaps, or scared, or simply needing him. He swung his arm under me as I let myself collapse into his arms.

He carried me over onto the grass only a few feet away from the water's edge and laid me down softly. I looked up at the sky and could see the outline of a burnt tree above my head. The beginnings of a shiver began creeping into me. Was it getting cold?

Peter laid his sweater over me. It seemed as if the winds had picked up and the sky was being painted colors. Those clouds weren't there before; the sky wasn't that shade of indigo.

I could see Peter looking around us, as if "help" would miraculously be there. Instead, I turned my head and saw it. There was a dead bird next to me. There was the Kingfisher: all black and silvery luminescent, and unmoving.

Closing my eyes, the pain became pervasive, like shock; I knew I needed something. "The bird..." I whispered. The shock of seeing Jung's painted bird there, lying next to me at that moment was the only thing in my mind. Somehow, if I could have that bird, I could be like the phoenix—I could be the one who could die and be reborn from her own ashes. I could be a phoenix. "I want it Peter. I want the bird!"

Peter looked down at me. He looked scared. He looked at the bird, then looked at me. The shivering got stronger. I closed my eyes tighter.

And then...it was as if I was beginning to see through my eyes: lights and shimmering mandalas were radiating through some deep darkness. And then they began looking like charts: There was Jung's chart, and mine...and Peter's chart—all appearing and disappearing, overlaying each other. There was my chart with my Sun, Neptune and Venus all clumped together, and then Peter's chart rising up into it like a developing photograph.

Peter's Neptune was radiating through my Venus: the symbol of idealism in love...had I ever told him that? And then Jung's mandala of a chart appeared—I could see his South Node, the astrological point of past life connection, like a bright star conjoining my Neptune and Venus. Why hadn't I seen this ancient connection before? Why hadn't I seen this hint of interconnected past lives? Why was my body quivering so much?

And then I felt him. Peter laid his warm body across mine...completely. The weight and heat from his body permeated mine like a warm comforter on a cold winter's day. I could feel the moisture from his breath and I breathed it in like an infusion to ease the shock.

The images of light and symbols began fading as I opened my eyes to Peter's soft gaze. To say I had never felt this before was obvious. But to say I had never seen such love in his eyes was true. It brought me back.

"The bird, Peter, please, get it...." He looked at me as if I had just told him to shoot me—as if I were a wounded horse asking to be shot. "Just wrap him up and we'll take him home."

And then he got up. I watched him as he walked over to the Kingfisher. He stood staring down at the mythological bird for a moment, and I wondered what he knew about it—if he knew that it carried both good and bad omens. Jung must have seen the bird on these same shores before he painted them on Philemon, his other-worldly mentor.

Peter bent over the dead bird but I couldn't see what he was doing at first. And then I saw—or heard—he was removing a wing. It had to be twisted off. Peter groaned a little. I squeezed my eyes shut and reminded myself that the bird couldn't feel pain.

And then I could feel the pain in my ankle return, but more than that, what I really felt was the weight of my body and the pull of the earth underneath me—like a magnet. I too was being pulled apart and I didn't know if I could release myself. I tried to control my breathing. I felt heavy, rooted here to this earth, wanting to be whole again. Yet I couldn't move. Maybe I too, was a dead bird. Were my wings were being torn off?

Peter walked back to me, and I felt his hand on my chest, gently rocking me, and calling my name. I opened my eyes. He slowly waved a long feather in front of my eyes.

"You did it!" My eyes could see every detail, and a little breeze moved the feathers. "It's like…a feather…a feather on the breath of God." He placed the feather in my hand.

Then he leaned over and kissed me on the forehead, then on the nape of my neck, and finally on my lips. It was so soft and pure, like the first time we ever kissed.

"Come. It's not meant for us to stay here any longer. Come…" and he scooped me up and carried me into the kayak.

In another hour we were back at the hotel, my ankle soaked with ice, my heart full and grateful. Why had this mattered so much? Why did it seem as if all that mattered now was Peter and the presence of a one small blue-black feather? Maybe heroic deeds happen in strange ways. What had been rescued?

"Called or not called, God is present." Jung's words—and a small heroic deed. A wounding and a flight...ah...we had approached the castle at Lindisfarne first by foot, and now Jung's stone retreat by water. We had claimed a victory and a little prize. A feather of hope. It felt like a good omen. But I knew I was scheduled to be on the flight back to the states tomorrow, and that didn't feel good. Would he ask me to stay on?

Chapter 17
The Sunday Afternoon Philosopher's Club

He didn't. The next day I returned home, alone. Peter was full of rational reasons why we should do it this way. Saturn delays, and sometimes disappoints. Peter had his ways and he took me to the airport and very "matter of factly" started saying good-bye. It wasn't unfriendly, just not what I was beginning to hope for, and he could tell that by my quietness.

"We've healed something between us, haven't we? So why do you always get so emotional about everything?" He asked.

"Am I being emotional?" I looked at him with my coldest stare. Then he kissed me good-bye. It was so tender, so civil, so proper, so restrained…so loving almost, but without any hint of passionate need. It had been years since we had truly come together sexually and maybe if we had done that—! Maybe if we had one afternoon of luscious love-making it would have been different.

I tried to smile. "It's true, I guess. I am impatient…. in manners of the heart." But then I steeled myself, turned away and walked through the airport gate. It felt as if Peter wasn't telling me everything.

I wanted a new beginning with him—damn it! I couldn't understand why he had to stay at this conference so much longer. He said he would be there at least two months more, probably three, since he had volunteered to do work for them there—he reminded me that he was getting free rent and board in exchange for working through to the end of their season. He was honoring his commitments, but his objectivity suggested he wasn't feeling any *wrenching-away* like I was. Or was he high on patience and low on money? I certainly couldn't afford to stay longer.

And so, I returned home, alone, the next day. It was sad—no, it was more than sad—it felt ominous leaving Peter at that moment. I had finally felt my heart opening towards him at Jung's retreat, but now it was closing again. How could he be so warm one minute and cool the next?

Sophie met me at the airport. No tears here, just hugs. She looked really happy, and I wondered if she was expecting some great news from me, about us. But there was going to be no news there. Sophie had been living with friends, but now she had "news" to tell me—she had been offered a job working as a waitress in a popular Irish Pub in New York City. She was going to take it for a little while, she said, and then maybe apply to art school there; maybe.

"Really, you're moving?"

"I've already moved—got a sweet little place just outside the city. I wanted to wait till you came back to tell you." I stood there shocked. "So how was your time with Dad? How was it? When's he coming back?" She beamed. "Do you have 'news'—I mean, did you guys decide…?" She gave me a knowing look.

"…waiting. We're waiting." Her smile dropped. "It was a great time, but, you know Peter, he doesn't like to rush into things." I tried to pretend happiness.

And so it went. I shared the story of our time together, as Sophie brought me back to my front door, to Charles Street, to my "home." We made tentative plans to come have her stay overnight with me soon. Then she left. Alone again…no amount of hugs and kisses good-by was going to change anything.

❧

As soon as I walked in the door at my Charles Street home, I felt Theo's absence. The usually cozy room felt cold and empty. Dead

And it was Sunday. A gray Sunday. But then I remembered—yes!—it was Sunday and it was the time of Thomas' Sunday Afternoon Philosopher's Club! I could go to the meeting and bring my beloved Theo home as well.

I hurriedly changed my clothes, threw a tiny box into a bag, and rushed out the door. A heavy mist lay over the rain-soaked city. I turned the corner off Charles St, and started making my way to Chestnut St, but found myself getting out of breath. The uneven brick sidewalks were unforgiving; I tripped on the curb.

And then my weakened ankle gave way as I went face down over an upturned brick and fell onto the sidewalk. Damn! Everything in my bag threw out onto the road. As I picked them up I kept thinking this is the part of the movie when the heroine cries and the music gets poignantly loud—or maybe like an old black and white movie. But there was no real drama here, just a trip-up. Get over it, I thought.

I had never been in Thomas' bookshop when it was actually open. Instead I had walked by and looked in the window one night after hours and delighted in seeing what I can only describe as the quintessential old bookstore, with low ceilings and a pleasant disheveledness. It was the kind of shop that is almost extinct, but it was still here and so was I.

I was actually out of breath by the time I arrived on the doorstep. I felt anxious…why was I nervous? I wanted to see Theo and Thomas. I wanted to belong somewhere, to some people, to some place. Perhaps I needed something or someone to come home to…and this was it.

Opening the latched door with an unsteady hand, I peered inside. I could smell pipe smoke and see the rough-hewn wooden beams across the old ceiling. Books were piled on the sales counter as before and overflowing in stacks on the floor. Thomas spotted me immediately.

As I pushed opened the heavy door, the door chimes announced my arrival. I could see Thomas running his hand through his wild white hair, giving his beard a little tug as if to wake himself up, and ambling over eagerly to greet me. He gave me a long hug. My thoughts shocked me: *I love this man—! Is this the way one might feel towards a truly loving father? When I see him I get a rush—a feeling that he wants to protect me, and that he's proud of me.... and he always has that twinkle in his eye when he sees me.*

And there he was again, radiant as always, with his easy manner and quick smile. He seemed taller, and his deep blue shirt made his thick white hair stand out even more. Yes, I thought, he looks like a French Impressionist painter—if there was such a "look." His casual clothes hid a strong robust body. When his arms encircled me, the warmth of his bear-like body infused me with goodness...like a shot of whiskey on a cold day—it literally warmed me all over.

And there, sitting in a circle were his friends, the Sunday philosophers. For some reason I couldn't help but think that each one of them sensed that he loved them in a special way...not in exactly the same way, but in a way that was uniquely special to each one of them. Perhaps I too, was falling under the charm of his charisma.

"Lovely to see you, my dear! Theo has missed you. I have too." It had only been five weeks I'd been gone.

It felt like years. "Come over and sit, my dear! What a surprise!"

He quickly introduced me to what he called "the usual cast of characters." Thomas announced their names and simply what they did for work. There was: Richard, a wine merchant (whose ruddy face suggested he loved his work), Carlos, the young Italian waiter from the corner cappuccino shop who I recognized immediately, Meredith, an antique shop owner from the Hill (whose thinness hinted of frailness and strictness), and Phillip, a professor from Boston University (whose tight collar and v-neck sweater pinched him, hinting of both confidence and vulnerability.)

They were sitting on old wooden chairs in the corner of the shop. Thomas, of course, wouldn't have described them as I saw them. I was a newcomer to the group, and I wasn't sure that they wanted another person there who might take away part of their personal time with their charismatic leader. Meredith was the only one who actually frowned at me.

Thomas sat down back down in his rocking chair and I couldn't decide if he looked more like a contented cat or a father on Christmas Eve sharing his beloved books with his children. He was so obviously the hub of the wheel here, the center and guru of this little group. He had a generosity of time to give, and the ability to listen, as well as a propensity to giving away his books. If you were in the "club" and interested in a subject, you'd find a book in your hand by the end of the afternoon, and there'd be no charge.

Thomas kept exclaiming how surprised he was to see me, as I hadn't told him exactly when I'd be back. Then Theo came over and curled around my feet. He had been allowed to wander around the shop freely, in my absence, and he looked more than content. He looked loved, and fat. I picked him up and stroked him thoroughly. Thomas made motions for me to sit down, so I did.

Phillip, who spoke with a slight English accent, must have decided to be the one to instruct me: "Isabelle, the topic for discussion today, is—you'll be happy to hear—from your favorite philosopher, Jung—the section in this book where he talks about how we must hold the tension of the opposites, till the third way appears—what he calls the reconciling third." Thomas must have told the group a little about me beforehand since Phillip knew I liked Jung. I wondered too if they knew I was an astrologer.

I stared out the window, thinking how Jung and astrology were once frowned upon in academic circles. I wondered if I would be accepted into this little group. Carl Jung was now accepted in academia, but astrology bears a threatening stamp of irrationality to it—especially to those of the academic persuasion, or to those who connect it with the allure of the gypsy underworld. It's a somewhat private language that is also disliked by some because it appears to give some people power.

In the past, those in political power usually choose to either quietly pay for their astrologers, or publicly burn them at the stake.

I mused: I could tell them how Jung was one of the first to use astrology in his practice with clients and to explore its symbolism, so he restored a "professionalism" to it—although he was highly discouraged in his exploration of the worlds of alchemy and astrology. I knew how it cost him many close relationships as well as a lot of personal pain. Some say that his closest friend, Toni Wolff, distanced herself from him because she couldn't stand his delving in these disreputable fields.

Meredith saw me spacing out and filled me in about last week: "Last Sunday we had a fabulous discussion about fierce grace. Thomas reminded us of how we need to consider whatever happens to us, as a kind of grace. Good or bad." I wondered what Meredith saw as her fierce grace? She certainly didn't look like she was in the bloom of grace or health.

So who were these people? Were they really a book discussion group, a philosophy discussion group, or a small gathering of groupies around their spiritual guru—?

"Grace?!" I exclaimed, as I bounced out of my musings, and came back into the moment. "Grace and patience: something I have very little of!" They laughed. I had no patience with anything nor 'grace' in love right now. *If only they knew how much I was truly trying to "hold the tension of the opposites" but my loneliness and my hope were pulling in different directions. Peter's decision to stay away—for an unknown amount of time, and Sophie's decision to move away altogether, certainly didn't feel like grace. More like abandonment. Was there a reconciling third? Could be my writing? I needed to come home to myself, and writing could be that anchor. Could I ever—ever—get the writing on Saturn into a finished book?*

I took a little package out of my bag and handed it to Thomas. "For you, for caring for Theo—"

"Ah, not necessary, as Theo has been caring for us. He's been charming the customers and making friends…" The crows-feet around Thomas' eyes turned upward into little smiles as he opened the package slowly and deliberately. At first he didn't understand what he was seeing.

I was proud of my gift. I had wandered around the old city of Zurich for hours that last day, in pursuit of the perfect gift for Thomas. Peter had returned to his Krishnamurti gathering in the mountains outside of Zurich, and I was yet again on my own. What I found was a small stone paperweight of the "forgotten stone" carved by Jung at Bollingen. It was square, about the size of a baseball, and carved on each side with Latin and Greek inscriptions as well as astrological symbols.

As Thomas un-wrapped the paper, I tried to explain: "I don't have a cross or a star as a symbol of my spirituality, or any talisman of this last journey—but this stone mandala comes pretty close. It's a copy of what's called the 'forgotten stone'—the stone that was left at Jung's house by mistake, by men who were delivering supplies from a quarry nearby to his home. He carved and sculpted it into this. It's huge actually…and I did see it when I was there….but long story short—he carved it in honor of his 75th birthday, and well…. Thomas, I thought of you when I saw it, and thought you might like it."

"It's a perfect gift, considering our topic of conversation today!" I wondered if I heard a touch of sarcasm there. Meredith, the antique shop owner, probably noticed that it wasn't even an antique reproduction, but—heaven forbid—a souvenir of sorts.

Thomas however, looked at it closely, caressing it with his fingers, as I continued explaining the curious cube: "You see on this side of it, it's a mandala divided into four; the number of wholeness. In the center is a little monk holding a lantern—it's called a 'homunculus,' which in ancient books, meant 'the little man inside the brain'. And if you look closer, you'll see that he has the astrological sign for Mercury on his robe."

Thomas interrupted: "Hermes! This is Mercury, same as the messenger-god Hermes, who's the one who mediates between the outer worlds and the inner worlds, and between the living and the dead. He's a hermit-monk- trickster all in one. He bridges "the worlds" and brings people and ideas together—like you, Isabelle!" I thought Thomas was more like Mercury than me.

Phillip looked curious and shot a question to Thomas: "You once told me that Mercury was like a rogue teacher, navigating between worlds, crossing thresholds into invisible worlds. You once told me I was like him, but I don't get it."

Meredith looked slightly annoyed: "We all have Mercury, Phillip, not just you. It's all about our style of communicating. Some astrologer told me where mine was...it was doing something bizarre...retrograding and all that. Oh, yes, she said mine was in Gemini, which she said was ruled by Mercury. Ruled? Can't imagine it."

I piped in: "Gemini is a sign, but Mercury is a planet. They're very similar and planets 'rule' signs, so Gemini is very curious, and can bridge the gap between "opposites." They are great open-minded communicators when they want to be. And, Gemini is known for having two sides, like two people, so sometimes you don't know who you're speaking with when you're talking with a person who has a lot of Gemini in their chart..."

Meredith lifted her eyebrows with a hint of disdain, and shook her head disapprovingly. I wasn't going to let her stop me.

"Look here—"I said, pointing to the stone, and hoping to move away from the jargon of pop astrology: "On the top here is the glyph for Saturn, and beneath it is the sign for Mars. These 'yang' signs are about the resistance of Saturn and the assertiveness of Mars."

Carlos looked up at Thomas: "I think I've got a lot of that Mars energy always being frustrated..." He chuckled. Carlos found a tiny piece of paper that came wrapped with the stone: "Look here—it says the Greek writing around the center says: 'The man in the center, the homunculus, is the one who traverses the dark places of the world…."

Thomas chuckled. "Hey, I think there's a little homunculus in there." He pointed to Carlo's open fly on his tight blue jeans. "Sometimes Mercury is about zipping up your fly! You know, you've got assertive Mars and cautious Saturn both in there…." He seemed to love to tease Carlos.

Carlos looked down and zipped up. "I don't get it." Carlos grinned and looked at Thomas for an explanation.

Thomas exhaled on his pipe, filling the room with a sweet fragrance."Astrology is a symbolic system—and confusing at first. But you could think of this Mercury as being a bit like that zipper there—when it goes up, it pulls together what has been separated—like those Mars and Saturn energies—and when it goes down, it opens what has been joined."

I chuckled to myself, remembering that this little comparison of Mercury to a zipper was something I had once told Thomas, as I had learned about Mercury from my teacher, a delightful Sophia-like woman, Alice Howell. She was one of those wise women who had inspired me over the years, and now I was impressed that Thomas remembered it.

Carlos looked at the zipper on his pants. "Well, when what's inside the zipper, goes up, well, I—certainly like to join together—but sometimes he's a trickster! So maybe I should call him, Mercury?" Carlos laughed and looked up at Thomas for approval.

Instead, Richard the wise-man of wine, snapped back: "Let's get serious now...really, there's something to learn here—it reminds *me* of the synapses in the brain, and how chemicals—anti-depressants—connect to the receptors on each side of the nerve. They zip them together." I wondered if he was taking "serotonin uptake inhibitors" for depression, or if he stayed with his wine drinking—another Mercurial substance that loosens the tongue.

"I don't believe in astrology, and I don't like drugs. I think we're getting off track here." Meredith snapped.

"But Meredith," Phillip added, "try thinking "out of the box" for a moment. Think how strange Mercury is—it's liquid silver! So slippery, yet it's in a thermometer that can read our temperature...and as a metaphor; I don't know...." *How interesting everyone interprets things according to what they know and feel, I thought.*

"Well, my temperature is getting a little bit hot, Phillip!" Meredith laughed at herself. "I didn't come here today to talk astrology; but to talk philosophy and Jung."

I gathered that she wasn't going to act from her open-minded " Mercury ruled Gemini." I have Mercury in Scorpio, but I wasn't going to challenge her. Then I had a strong intuition that she was a Cancer—Cancers love antiques and touching into the traditions of the past. And they can be quite moody and cranky when they want to be—looney types even; their sign being ruled by the ever changing Moon.

I could understand how she felt. I wouldn't believe in astrology either if I hadn't studied it and used it, and found that it simply worked. If it was all just simplified down to "sun sign astrology" as it is in the newspapers, it would be as valid as a fortune cookie. But the chart is so complex with all its signs and houses and aspects—it truly reflects how paradoxical we all are.

Thomas looked tense. I could see him closing his eyes as if he were looking inside for an answer to comfort his children...his students.

"Meredith, could you look at it the way Jung did? Jung said, somewhere in this book, that we are each like grapes in a vineyard that was grown in a particular place and in a particular year and season in time. And astrology is like that—it uses the birth time and place—so you are like a wine-grape that comes from a section of France perhaps, in a particular year, and therefore you take on the characteristics of that time and place."

"You mean I'm like a fine wine that gets better as it ages?" The eternal feminine hope, I thought.

"Yes, exactly." Thomas had come to my defense! I loved it. It gave me confidence to go just a little further—

I thought how Thomas was acting like Mercury by creating this group—by getting us together to connect what had been torn apart or separated within each of our psyches. He brought us all together.

If ever I was to connect with them, it would be now. So I took a deep breath and went on: "Together the planets in the four quadrants of the mandala here tell a story. Jung believed all "the opposites in our nature", even of good and evil, were intimately related and inseparable. He felt God and man needed each other, in a sense, to be whole." I was surprised I remembered that much off the top of my head.

Thomas touched my hand as if to "second" what I had said. I felt a little unnerved, because I didn't understand this unspoken gesture. But he simply said: "Go on...."

"Well, that's it really...." But then in my enthusiasm I told them about visiting Jung's house and the mythological Kingfisher bird. It was as if I was trying to understand it all, but instead, as the afternoon moved on, it seemed as if everything became a blur. I must have jet lag, I thought, or overtiredness.

I was the last to leave. Thomas gently stroked Theo one more time: "I'll miss you little guy." Then he lifted Theo into the cat carrier, and led me to the door. As he handed Theo over to me, Thomas tilted his head and looked at me as if he wanted to ask me something.

"You going to be alright, now? Being alone now and all?" His eyes widened and I could feel his concern. I didn't say anything. Then he leaned over, and with a slight pause, kissed me on the lips. It was a gentle kiss but long and lingering. His hand held my cheek.

I was shocked and thrilled all at once. Underneath a certain fear, I felt happy, really happy, as if I had finally come home to someone. Was it to Thomas? Or was it to myself because I had dared to speak my truth to this group of 'philosophers'?

"Be well, my dear. Be well." I let my head fall on his chest, and he lightly stroked his hand across my hair. A wave of exhaustion or surrender came over me. Was this the hand of that underworld god, Pluto, urging me to surrender and let go? His hand on my head felt like a blessing. Pluto, Mercury, whatever, I didn't care.

"And now....come by again....soon. Yes?" He didn't move to close the door, and I didn't move down the step. I didn't want to go, and I didn't want to stay. I wanted to curl up like Theo and sleep...and yet every inch of me was alive and vibrating. At that moment it felt as if Thomas needed me as much as I need him. But there was nothing to do, nowhere to go. It was all I could handle at the moment. I hugged him tight for a second, slipped out the door, and didn't look back.

Walking the few blocks home felt even foggier than when I had come. But different. I unlocked my door and gently set Theo down in the green rocker. He seemed to be happy enough. What was I feeling? Theo could be comfortable anywhere, unlike me.

I made a cup of tea, and paced around the rooms as if there was some way I could absorb all the confusion of emotion. It felt as if the room had changed. I was here only a few hours ago—had anything changed? My one flowering plant had completely died of dehydration. That would have to wait till tomorrow. But the rooms felt permeated with something, and I couldn't help but feel it was like a ghost or whiff of love. Something not tangible, yet real. Was Thomas my 'Reconciling Third?' I wanted a sense of wholeness to come forth from my writing, my work, my family….not another man, not Thomas—such a mercurial man!

But who knew if "the gods" had another idea in mind for me? Perhaps Sophia—the feminine spirit of wisdom and maker of all kinds of 'magic' and synchronicities….perhaps she knew more than I did here. Tomorrow I would spend the day writing. Maybe Sophia as writing muse or Sophie as daughter would come for a visit. Or maybe Peter could reach out across the miles and touch my heart in some way. I was open to all possibilities.

Chapter 18

Mirroring: "As Above, So Below."

Kendra@gmail.com

Dear Kendra~

Sounds like you've been going through hard times—like Sophie—your parents separating, your relationship with your boyfriend ending. Very similar…oh, I wish I could be like the mythological Merlin, magically bestowing answers and comfort, but instead, you have me, your friend, who is more humbly "a reluctant astrologer." But if I were Merlin, I would be sharing with you how the Soul has such strange ways of mirroring the ancient esoteric saying: "that which is above to that which is below." I would add too, that one is not to fear the dragons in the forest, but that the dragons in the psyche need be loved and appeased first.

You have serious questions about the "shadow side" of astrology. You see that there appears to be many ways to make astrology "prove anything" because there are different ways of approaching this art. It's true I don't see astrology as a science, with definitive rules but a more intuitive and synthesizing art.

So, this mystery of astrology is illusive at times—with its "smorgasbord" of systems, or dialects—-it doesn't present a united front. The different systems are the 'shadow quality' of our work for sure. But there are two things that are important to remember: all astrology is here to remind us that we are part of a larger cosmos, plan and purpose, and that we can trust in a pattern that is greater and wiser than ourselves. People need to know that. They need to see how their particular story is part of a larger sacred story. And I believe, as the ancient Hindu's believed, that "Goodness" exists at the heart of it.

We go to astrology so we can make better choices—and we want to know about ourselves without someone pathologizing, shaming or blaming us. We want to understand why we do what we do, and astrology—no matter what "dialect system" it uses—gives us a way to talk deeply about ourselves and our inner struggles.

You asked about the different "language dialects" between systems—-such as the Vedic vs the Western approach, or the different house systems such as Placidus vs Koch....well, I think most astrologers are simply drawn to a teacher who uses a particular method, and who shows them that it works. And then they find a way to work within that language system as well.

Astrology is a language and in a language a "table is a table" whatever we name it in any language. A planet symbol exists, like a table exists, so it's ironic when someone says "I don't believe in astrology because I then feel like saying: You don't believe in Spanish or French either?

And of course, just because one person primarily uses the birth chart and asteroids and another relies on planetary progressions and transits, doesn't make any of them wrong or better. It's a language that speaks to the Soul, and different dialects speak clearer to some people more than others. The ideal in any astrological system is to be able to see a theme repeated several times in different ways—sometimes called the rule of three: you see a theme repeated three times, you know that what it points to carries weight....some truth.

So not only are systems, orbs, aspects, and "readings" not perfect "black and white" paradigms, but people, like their charts, are often profoundly paradoxical! Like the planets that are held within the mandala of the chart, people have many sub-personalities, and are constantly in the process of changing as well! What underlies a good reading of a chart has much less to do with the mechanics of the astrologer's technique than something else—something most astrologers use almost unconsciously..what is it?

I think we want a synchronistic moment of "ah-ha!" when there's been an accurate mirroring of that which is above to that which is below—when the client's story and the astrologer's explanation of the symbolism rise up to a little epiphany together. There's a match...a felt moment of synchronicity between the chart and the personal story that makes all considerations of proof of technique secondary. This "magic of synchronicity" is the essence of an astrological reading. Perhaps that is our only safeguard in truth-seeking; not forcing our predictions or symbolism or bias on anyone, but honoring instead the idea that we are acting as Hermes did—as a translator of the symbols and a communicator.

When we're looking at this blueprint of the psyche, we're looking for those little moments...for what the Jungians call 'numinous moments' when we look to see the answers projected there…when the god within and the god above are resonating.

Ah…I feel like I'm waxing a bit poetic here—but you got me going! Hope this helps~

With Love,

~Isabelle

ক

<u>*Kendra@gmail.com*</u>

Dear Kendra~

Two emails in one day—so what? You're right about being concerned about what I told you before about Thomas. Yes, all that Pluto in his chart is a bit unnerving! But don't worry about me. I know that Pluto can be ruthless, yet this Pluto, this "God of the Underworld" is somewhere in everyone's birth chart—and it's always busy "revolutionizing" by clearing away the old and making room for the new.

I think Thomas' strong Pluto in his birth chart reveals his deep vulnerability, fear…and his strength.(Did I tell you he keeps fingering his Celtic cross as we talk? It's his talisman, I guess.) In mythology, Pluto wore a helmet that made him invisible, and as you may remember he stole Persephone and brought her to the underworld as his wife. It's a strange story really—about a young woman losing her innocence, leaving her mother, and spending half the time in the underworld with Pluto, and the other half of her time in the above-world with her mother, Demeter.

BTW, did you know that Pluto has been demoted from a planet? I think it's because of its tiny size (but astronomers don't know it's the most powerful 'planet' in astrology) and

Demeter, who was discovered in 1801 and proclaimed to be a planet orbiting between Mars and Jupiter, has been demoted to a "dwarf planet" or asteroid as well. Demeter, or Ceres is one of the archetypes of the Mother. Ah...astronomers underestimate the power of these archetypal gods!

Now they just discovered a new celestial body out beyond Pluto called Eris or Xena. Like the film goddess, Xena, she's about the female warrior spirit, probably because she's in the constellation of assertive Aries. Astrologers don't know what to make of this new planet yet, because the meaning of the discovery of a planet always reflects something of the meaning/zeitgeist of the times. Some astrologers feel that Eris/Xena reflects both the chaos of this time in history and the warrior spirit of women's struggle against patriarchy and pornography.

You asked too about science and astrology—sometimes the mix is like oil and water...they are both repelled by each other. But history and astrology is another thing. They correlate in tandem, as the meaning of each new planet always reflects the nature of the time it's discovered...as when revolutionary Uranus was discovered in the 1700's we had both the American and French revolutions. When Pluto was discovered in the 1930's we discovered Plutonium and the atomic bomb that later figured into World War II.

So, now we have Uranus, the awakener and the revolutionary "squaring off" to Pluto in Capricorn—Pluto as a sleuth will sniff out corruption in corporations, banks, and structures that are unsound. Pluto will "occupy them" till they change. And who knows how this newly discovered planet beyond Pluto will affect us? Who knows how this newly discovered archetypal "woman" beyond Pluto may impact our lives now....?

But to answer your question about Thomas' character: I don't know whether it's good to judge anyone too much by looking at their chart, as we don't know how a person has acted out these energies. Being born with a lot of Pluto, like Thomas, can mean he was subject to a lot of trauma in life. But it doesn't mean he was guilty or bad in any way because of it! In fact, with Pluto it's really a victory to not fall into feeling like the victim, but to surrender to the story and heal. Many therapists have a strong Pluto—it's like having a stamp on your passport, saying you've "been to hell and back". You could say with Pluto: "What doesn't kill me makes me stronger."

And then there's Saturn. It seems as if astrologers either want to make light of Saturn transits, or tend to make them the opposite—fearful. I lean towards seeing the positive restructuring that Saturn wants to build, but I'm aware that it's a mistake to turn the darkness of Cronus (Saturn) into too much of a good thing—for this would miss the fact that what appears to be the dark night of the Soul still is dark even though it can the awakening of imagination...and compassion. Before movement, there is no movement, just stuckness.

Both Peter and Thomas are strong men, each in their own way. I'm holding my Saturnian loneliness and yearning with all the "unknowing" of what's going to happen—-trying to hold the tension of the opposites and waiting for the way to be clear—till the third way is revealed. I am attempting to do that. Not easy.

Fondly,
Isabelle

As I looked up from writing to Kendra about Xena and about my perpetual waiting for Jung's "Reconciling Third Way" Thomas unexpectedly appeared at the door. I let him in, and as I did, he saw the tears in my eyes. I collapsed into my own counseling chair—

"Something's wrong, isn't it? Thomas sat down and took my hand in both of his. "You can tell me… Isabelle….we don't have to stay in any roles here. Just tell me what's happening."

"Thomas—tell me, if Peter meant what he said about our story not being over, why doesn't he come here? Why does he keep me waiting? He doesn't even email me. Sophie doesn't either. What's happening? I can barely stand what I'm feeling. How can I "hang in there" when the two people I love most in the world are barely communicating with me. I don't get it. Sometimes I feel like an angry sadness wants to take hold of me."

"Isabelle, Peter said he was coming, didn't he? You called him. So…. he has to finish whatever he's doing in Zurich, and I'm sure he'll be here as soon as he can."

Thomas took my hand as we sat down, knowing that those words were just like platitudes.. His head dropped. For a moment we simply sat there and didn't say anything. When he looked up I could see his eyes were closed.

"Heavenly Father….Divine Mother" he began. "We ask your help and support for Isabelle. We ask that her way be made clear and that she feel the Spirit of God within and around her. Let her know she is loved, and that your Love always will always answer her every human need. Grant her peace…"

Thomas' large hands were cradling and holding mine. There was energy here—it felt as if we had a direct line to God. No interference or static, just warm energy encircling us, and my mind flashed to Sophie's healing circle of prayer at Lindisfarne. A great wave of peace came over me. Thomas was here with me now. Maybe this healing was all I needed. Maybe he was what I needed.

Thomas looked me in the eyes: "Do not doubt the rightness of the two sides within you, and let whatever may happen, happen. A life without inner contradiction and tension is either only half a life or a life in the Beyond, which is destined only for angels. But God loves human beings more than the angels….Amen."

"Amen" I whispered, and let it all sink in. "Wait! Didn't Jung say that?" I finally asked.

"Exactly—I memorized it. There's more to it, but that's the part that stays with me. I'm so sorry my dear, about what's happening, but I guess I dropped by at the right moment, yes?"

"Yes….perfect timing." I'm struck by the synchronicity of Thomas quoting Jung to me just after I wrote to Kendra using Jung's ideas. I want Kendra to see the paradoxes of people and astrology without being judgmental. Here I am: both a "wise woman" and a "suffering woman"—sad, mad and waiting. And now, somewhere in there, I see that Thomas is in the equation too.

"And tomorrow…you'll come by again?" I asked.

He nodded, and grinned as he walked to the door.

I walked back to my computer and there was a shock: an email from Sophie—she suggested coming for a visit next week. Maybe the healing will continue. Maybe what has been unconscious will finally become conscious.

Chapter 19

"My Barn having burnt to the ground, I can now see the Moon." Zen quote.

It was a bright Tuesday morning when I met Sophie outside the Boston airport in a taxi. She looked so healthy, and I barraged her with questions immediately. "How did it go with your new job? Are you exhausted?"

"Great! I love New York...the work, everything." She seemed genuinely eager and happy to see me. It was going to be so sweet to have Sophie stay overnight with me, at my place, and see it for the first time. And despite the sounds of sirens and the bustling push of the city, I had begun feeling that the city's arms held me in a way they hadn't before.

"And your book? How's it coming?" she asked.

"It's finished, I think. Now I need to gather my courage to send it out." How do you know when a book is finished? I thought. Or a relationship finished? I hadn't heard from Peter since I returned, except for a one sentence email from him wanting to know if I made it home safe. He signed it, "With love, Peter." I guess he thought that was enough. I replied to him in one sentence that I was fine, just fine. and now it had been three weeks since we last spoke or wrote.

The taxi inched along, rounding the corner of the Public Gardens onto Charles Street, but there was a traffic snarl slowing us down. We could see in the distance that Charles St was cordoned off by police cars and the driver asked us if he could drop us off at the corner.

"Of course," I said, as we poured out of the taxi into a massive flow of people walking towards us; away from whatever calamity had just happened. The police opened just enough space to let the fire-engines leave. This was bizarre. Something had happened right near the corner where I lived.

We pushed on through the crowd coming at us. My stomach began tightening as a profound sense of disbelief and denial starting rising in me. I felt nauseous—whatever had happened was too close to home. I could now see orange barrior lines like angry flags draped across the street, and across the front of my apartment building. What was happening? What had happened?

I bumped into the side of a cop rushing past me. "Need to stay away from here—both of you!" he growled at us and kept going.

"But I live here!" I yelled, steeling my determination. Sophie had slowed down. I grabbed her arm and pushed past the last of the stragglers who had come to see the spectacle. It had been quite a fire, I heard someone say.

Started so slowly, just a small trail of black smoke rising from the left corner of the building. Nobody thought it would amount to anything. But the firemen had a hard time finding the right angle to shoot their hoses, and it took hours to drench the place sufficiently.

Heavy wooden cross planks covered my once blue door. My door! Water was still seeping out from under it, and the sidewalk was strewn with the insides of the building. The large front window was broken open—jagged glass edges protruded. And there on the sidewalk was a pile of shattered ceiling tiles, and my desk! My Larkin desk was propped up against the building looking like a crippled homeless person.

Sophie stopped, repelled by the scene. I thought I might throw up.

And there was Thomas, in the distance with Carlos. He hadn't seen us approaching, but I could recognize his white hair, with his arm holding one bag over his shoulder, and the other arm around a cat. He had saved Theo! Carlos and Thomas were talking animatedly and seemed to be walking away fast. I started running in their direction, then stopped. Thomas doesn't know I'm here, I thought, and my cell has been off. I didn't need to worry about Theo. I stood frozen in my bad dream, staring at my home, my study, my sanctuary. My refuge was now burnt, drowned, and split in pieces.

I slowly turned and walked back to Sophie. She was focused on her cell phone.

What was she doing? I had thought that being here with Sophie for a few days would be a way for her to see me in a new light, to reconnect—to share with her a bit of who I am now. We would sit in the warm amber light of my room, in the green velvet rockers—and she would somehow find me again amid all my things. But now all that was gone. And then I remembered that it was only last night I had written in my journal: "We do not live by things, but by the *meanings* of things in our lives." What was the meaning of this? This looked like a cosmic test of my sincerity.

Suddenly I came to my senses. What could be still salvaged from the fire? I could feel a rage of adrenaline rush through me as I thought of all I would lose. All those things that held my memoires...all those things...I fingered the door key in my pocket. I needed to get inside and retrieve them. The crowd and police were at a slight distance—just enough distance for me to go for it! Without another thought I bolted for the door, though I almost knocked Sophie over as I pushed right past her. Crouching down under the wooden beams, I lunged against the door with the full weight of my body. It didn't open. It was still locked, but I had my key ready in my pocket. Somehow I pushed the key into the hole, and I forced open the door.

I knew I only had seconds before I'd be caught. I breathed in the cold dank smell. I'd never smelled anything like that—like the taste of a dirty wet sponge in my mouth. There was blackness everywhere—-no amber light here! Books were toppled over, and ceiling tiles were hanging low under the weight of the water. Water was weeping in through the cracks as I heard another ceiling tile fall into a heap behind the stairway.

I skimmed the room. What had I come to save? The wrought iron face of the goddess in the fireplace remained untouched, her eyes looking downward, telling no secrets, sharing no stories of devastation. I spun around and reached for the large tin box that held old photographs of Peter and Sophie, my journal, and my hard copy book. These mattered, and these all looked secure in their box. Thank God! These where what I had come for! Oh, and the laptop—thank God it had been shut down and closed, and that corner of the room looked intact.

I could see two policemen rushing towards me as I squeezed back through the door. Sophie threw herself between them and me—"She's coming out, she's out! Let her be!" she yelled at them. And grabbing my arm this time she pulled me away from the building.

With one hand she dismissed them, and with the other hand she shoved her cell phone at me. She grabbed the box and laptop from my arms. "It's Dad—I just called him. He wants to know if he should come—do you want him to come?" I was dazed and speechless. "Do you want him to come or not?" Sophie screamed at me.

I took the phone. "Peter? This is you?" Sophie glared at me, as all she could hear was a long pause, and see my confused face. "You would come?" Another pause. "Yes," I replied. "Yes, Peter, come…." I handed her back the phone.

He's coming I told her, as if she hadn't heard.

"Of course he's coming Mom! He wouldn't *not* come. He loves you. And if there's one person who will hang in there with you through this hell, it's him. But why did you run in there like a crazy person—what's this?" She pointed to the box.

I opened the lid. "These are my journal, my photographs, the book, and letters—from Kendra."

"You ran in there to get those? Really?" Her hands caressed the old-fashioned photograph album with the photos of her and Peter on the cover. And these?" She saw the printed out emails to and from Kendra.

I watched as Sophie's face turned into a curious smile. "I know about these." She touched the letters.

"But you don't. These are copies of the email letters from Kendra. We've been writing to each other about our lives…and astrology. Sometime, if you're ever interested, I could read some to you."

"Mom, I am Kendra."

No, I shook my head sadly.

"No, Mom really. I am Kendra. I made her up—I told you she was my friend, but she's me. I did it so I could write to you, so I could get to know who you really are—not just as your daughter. At first, I was too mad at you for leaving Dad to even talk, but then I got curious, and had the idea that I could create an email person—this fictitious Kendra. Then I could hear your side of things, and you could write to me without knowing it was me."

What? It was hard to believe that this Scorpio daughter of mine had been so—so—devious? Clever? Caring enough to do this? It was unbelievable almost, but so was everything else.

"You are Kendra?" I stared at her blankly.

She laughed. "Yes!" I could tell she was delighted. "I never told you, but I've been studying astrology for quite a while, and I didn't want to tell you because... well, I didn't want to be overly influenced by you. After you moved away from Dad and home I wanted to get to know you—who you really are, not just as my Mom."

"Really? My God, that was sneaky Sophie! And you pretended you were older..."

"....yup. But—I really have been using astrology—*and* I'm still a Christian. *And* I've been thinking about all you wrote about Saturn and astrology—*and* I'm fascinated about something else too—about: *Chiron.* Do you know about it? The little asteroid planet...the one that looks like a "key" in the chart? Chiron is the wounded healer in all of us. I was going to tell you this sooner or later, just didn't know it would be like this—here, now."

I felt surprised and pleased. I was at a loss for words.

Then her mood changed. She looked again at the picture of her and Peter on the cover of the photograph album. And then I saw the "little girl" look in her face again, wanting reassurance. "I didn't know you cared that much about me, and Dad." Her eyes filled with tears.

I reached out for her and held her tight. I could feel a great peace come over me, as if layers of "holding on" seemed to be falling away. It seemed as if my heart was breaking open—wide enough for all of them—Peter, Sophie, Thomas and even this "Kendra," this daughter of mine who was the holder of my sacred illusions.

I didn't care any more about their stories: the literal facts of what they were doing or why. I cared only for the fact that I loved each of them no matter what, and that it didn't really matter what happened or what they were doing or what they believed in....there was nothing to prove or defend anymore. Whether we were together or apart was secondary to the deeper truth that they were embedded in my heart. It seemed as if an "amber light" had been turned on inside of me now, and it was not in "my room"—it was safely in my heart, and that was all that mattered.

Chapter 20

"This is serious," said Pooh. "I must have an escape."
~A.A. Milne

I had spent the morning on the phone talking with the insurance adjustors about the fire, and started sifting through a couple of boxed remnants that the fireman had salvaged. Sophie had been encouraging and wanted to help more, but there wasn't much she could do. I suggested she should go off and take care of her personal errands for a bit, and leave me alone to ponder. I would be alright, I protested, but I knew I was still trying to digest everything that happened. I moved slowly and found myself just staring, out the window, looking at the clear blue sky. Nothing had changed in the world, but everything had changed for me.

The insurance adjustors had wanted to meet me, so I drove over to Charles Street from the hotel Sophie and I had rented for that night, and the next morning I was allowed back into my old rooms to see what else could be salvaged. The smell of the moldy water-logged rooms was creepy. There was no electricity—dankness permeated the rooms. I started to rummage about, looking beneath a few soggy items, but I couldn't do it. It was an overwhelming project of personal ruin.

But then I saw it—the painting of the "Fortune Teller." It had fallen down behind piles of wall board and broken plaster. There were deep gashes in the canvas, and the crushed frame had ripped apart one side. It was unredeemable. I felt weak. Yet I was surprised I hadn't thought about the painting before now. I hadn't seen it and so somehow had forgotten about it. How could I forget this?

What mattered to me now? How could I just forget this painting that had once been so important to me; it would live inside me now. I had the urge to run—instead I grabbed a few "dry" astrological books and rushed back outside. Suddenly I could breathe. Nothing more was salvageable as far as I was concerned.

The insurance men and "fire/damage cleanup" crew were standing around with their coffees and all the reports of statistics and damages in hand. I signed off the last of the papers so they could begin their work, and thanked them profusely.

As I started rushing back to my car, I could feel that I was holding back a feeling—what was it? There was nothing more to do or say, there was neither hope or despair, nor regret or remorse. Yes, like in the Japanese saying: my barn having been burned to the ground, I could now see the moon. Perhaps.

And then I saw them. Thomas and Carlos were walking on the other side of the street. I saw them stop and face each other—the way people sometimes do when they stop at an important point in their conversation. They were looking at each other so intensely, but then Carlos started waving his hands in the air as if to explain something he couldn't find words for…I could see Thomas putting his hand on Carlos' shoulder. And then, it was almost as if Carlos' body diminished beneath the weight of Thomas' hand.

I crossed the street. They saw me approaching them. Carlos quickly wiped his eyes and pretended not to see me as he turned and walked away, up the hill at a fast pace. Thomas stood staring at him and then he looked at me. Thomas looked spent, and more disheveled than usual, with his shirt hanging out of his pants on one side, and his face looking red and roughened.

I vaguely remember walking over to him and smiling with a false cheerfulness. I remember walking back to his bookstore with him and thanking him for saving Theo. I remember asking Thomas if he would like to keep Theo if he wanted him…or at least to keep him till I got resettled. He agreed. I remembered us asking each other how we were doing and how tired our faces looked. Finally I asked him about Carlos, and this I remember word for word.

Thomas sucked in his lips and shook his head. "Don't know about him. It's the 'same old, same old' thing. He wants more than I can give him. Long story—but you? I mean—you must be…devastated?" I looked around his bookstore at all his things.

"No, for some reason I'm not." Yet I remember hoping he'd suggest some way to make it all better for the moment. Like maybe hand me his current favorite self-help book or suggest lunch. But he didn't. Instead he looked down at his hand.

And then I saw it. He had a new mark on his hand. It was a small version of the larger Celtic tattoo that Carlos had on his arm. He saw me looking at it, and shoved his hand into his pocket. Why was he hiding this?

"So, what's happening with you?" I asked, hoping he'd tell me some version of his truth at the moment.

"Nothing really. Same old, same old."

"Really?" I said. So he wasn't going to tell me. Was this the tendency of his Venus-Pluto that I'd seen in his chart—the aspect that tends to get into triangular or complicated emotional situations?

"Oh, I've been meaning to tell you that I have to go to my sister's house. She apparently needs me for something. She's getting on there in years, you know, she's near ninety. So there's no meeting this Sunday. I'm going out to the Cape. Not sure how long I'll be gone for, but I can take Theo. Sorry I can't be here for you now."

"Really?" I said again. I was surprised that "really" was the only word that I could find to say. What was the reality I was inquiring about? At least he was making my feelings about him easier. If he couldn't tell me the truth of whatever was going on between him and Carlos, or even between us, well, that said it all for me.

"I'm sorry, my dear, about all that's happened with you...your shop and all. But...I'm glad you have your daughter, and Peter—will he be coming back to help you?"

"Yes, but..." I shrugged my shoulders. I looked him directly in the eyes but he quickly looked away.

He continued: "Yeah, I need to get away from here for a bit. Close up shop for a bit . Are you going to re-open here? I just walked by your shop with Carlos—we went away for a couple of days together, and got back just in time to see the fire. Unbelievable." He waved his hand in the direction of my ruins. "Damn pity, really. How are you doing?" He repeated.

"I'm going to miss you." That was all I remember saying. Maybe he had been the reconciling third for me in my healing, but he wasn't going to be the literal third in my love life.

I had the strong sense that Thomas was never coming back. There would be reasons: none of them really true. And he did protest: "I've got to get away, you know. Business is down. Everything is what...what do you call it? Too much. Too much Pluto...too much Pluto-Venus...you know." Then he smiled at me, and I caught a glimpse of the Thomas I had once known. "Life spins us around in strange ways, at times, eh? Maybe God wants to know what our real intentions are, and if we're actually going to use our spiritual muscles to 'walk our talk' as they say…" he added.

I looked at a more complicated Thomas than I'd ever seen before. I didn't care that much about whatever may or may not have been happening with Carlos or any of those 'Sunday Afternoon Philosophers'—what mattered to me was that it felt like I was losing someone who was so very close to my heart; someone who had been there for me when no one else was.

"Good luck with your sister, Thomas. We can still be in touch, can't we?" I put out my hand coolly to shake his—he hugged me instead. "I'm sorry."

"Me too…" I said, feeling weak. Then we stepped back from each other, and just stood there, looking at each other. Thomas stared down and sighed. I thought I've never seen him look so old and tired before.

My head was swirling: What had been going on in his life? Who was I to him? What had he been for me? Simply a friend or a true spiritual mentor? I had made him into someone who carried the image of the loving father, the wise man, the eccentric artist…and maybe even lover.

Thomas had filled a place in my psyche no one else could ever fill. He had that quality of charisma that people get seduced into projecting on—they'd love him, hate him, talk about him…all that. I wondered if the weight of carrying all that for so many of us have finally become too much for him?

Don't I carry some of that energy in myself? I had often carried the projection of the "one who knows" as an astrologer. But the thought of Thomas and Carlos being so close, possibly lovers, was an uncomfortable one to digest. Yet I had no more right to claim him than anyone else. Maybe he had to move away from me—and Carlos. Maybe he knew what he was doing. That was a more comforting thought. Still, I couldn't get away from feeling as if he was betraying me, and he knew it.

"Isabelle..." He leaned back against the brick building behind him as if he were out of breath, and then looked past me at the strangers passing us along Charles Street. Sometimes even home can feel alien. "What can I say?" He voice quivered slightly. "It's up to you now to decide how you're going to feel about us..."

I didn't move. He was right. He was no more betraying me than I was betraying him. I was going to be meeting up with Peter again. I was going to be making a decision for myself. I simply hadn't gathered in all the pieces yet; all the threads of confused feelings.

In truth, I had never wanted to see Thomas clearly in the first place. One could even say I had been using him, if only in my mind—I had begun to see him in so many ways, but he was most like the wise messenger between worlds: Mercury. And Mercury connects and disconnects, joins and unjoins. Mercury can be a trickster. The only choice now was how we were going to tell ourselves the story of who we were to each other.

He reached into his jacket pocket, retrieved something, and held it out to me.

"Here. Would you keep this...for you...for us?" Open in the palm of his hand were the wooden mala prayer beads that I so often saw him fingering. They were worn and used, like he was. I nodded my head, as he slipped the mala beads around my wrist.

"They've got that God-connection, you know—might come in useful sometime." He grinned. So these would be our connection now. Oh yes, I still loved him. And because I did love him, I did what the old songs tell us to do: I let him go.

Chapter 21

> "Love doesn't sit there like a stone, it needs to be made, like bread; remade all of the time, made new." ~Ursala LeGuin

I drove to New York later that day, in a daze, to Sophie's new place. She would be coming home from work later tonight and Peter was scheduled to arrive in a few hours—what would I feel seeing him again? Perhaps I would feel his love? Or his coolness? Would he want to help me now? I was afraid to hope anymore.

But I could feel the fear of hope. I reminded myself that I was not the victim of anything except divine intervention with that fire, and who knows, that might be good. Maybe I needed to let go of my illusions—all that holding on to Thomas and to "my sanctuary." What really mattered to me wasn't the "stuff" there, but a feeling.

What was that feeling? It was a loss for sure, because "things" are more than they seem. They hold the past, they show what we once thought was valuable or beautiful, and they speak of our hopes and fantasies for who we are now and who we hope to become. I could hold a gift in my hand and feel the memory of the person who gave it to me, or I could hold an old sweater or scarf and remember the night I first wore it.

The loss of my home was the loss of a sense of place, a feeling of a safe and familiar harbor, and of a mood that warmed my heart. Its cozy Victorian ambiance was something I found comfort in—but who knows if I had ever lived in that time of not? I certainly didn't know. But I resonated with something from that era, with something in the way the afternoon sunlight shone in through the tiny paned windows, the way the high ceilings made me feel spacious, and the way a hand-crafted fireplace with a carved mantel could hold the essence of a room. It was the center point, not a television. Those were the times when women wore their hair high in a bun on top of their heads and men tipped their hats when a woman they knew walked by. That felt good to me.

But none of this now was as important to me as the people who were truly a part of my life, and the times I had once lived in. I had lived on Beacon Hill in a time when women wore long skirts and dresses, when men wore long hair and beards, and when there was a feeling of enchantment in the air. We knew we lived in a special time. And I was not so naïve that I didn't know I was trying "to come home again" and contrary to popular euphemisms, I had done just that. But now it had all gone up in smoke. What was important was that I had come home to something in myself. I could and would rebuild my dream. Some deaths imply a resurrection, and this one certainly did for me.

And so, I decided that I was going to trust that whatever happened tonight between me and Peter tonight was going to be alright. There would be no more back and forth between us—I couldn't stand that anymore. I could stand by myself, or I could stand with Peter. So much depended on what he would say tonight and how I would feel about it. That simple.

When I got back to Sophie's place I collapsed on her couch. I tried to meditate, and then gave up and made a pot of Earl Gray tea. I took out a couple of Peter's pottery mugs, poured my tea, and waited. I wondered if he'd be late. Here I was again in that hell of an in-between place and it wasn't fun. I looked down at my wrist and fingered the prayer beads. Yes, they were a comfort.

I walked around Sophie's apartment in circles, and finally sat down with my laptop. There were all the charts again—the astrological aspects for the fire, for Mother's funeral, for leaving Peter, and even for now. I wasn't surprised to see a harsh aspect between Mars and Uranus at the time of the fire, forcing me to release attachments to the material world. Saturn was just leaving it's conjunction to my Sun, and I wasn't surprised to see Jupiter there too—opening up new opportunities and freedom. I felt the paradoxical need to both surrender and to act: to honor the inevitability of Pluto change and the desire of Saturn to restructure life.

I glanced past the computer and let my eyes sweep across Sophie's books. What a strange mix of books! Some Christian inspirational writers, a few novels, Celtic mythology, and a rather large collection of astrology books. The books looked like they had all been well read. I opened one and it was underlined and coffee stained. Yes, she certainly had me fooled with pretending to be "my mentee!" My Kendra.

There was a book open on the shelf I hadn't seen before: it was on Chiron. I had never understood Chiron, or used it in my readings. Apparently it's a strange little astrological symbol that looks like a key—a "planetoid" between the two major opposing planets of Saturn and Uranus. The book said that most astrologers don't use Chiron, because it's not a major planet, but according to the author, it has quite a story to tell us.

I kept reading: "In mythology, Chiron was a centaur, half man and half horse, who was the son of Saturn. He was often known as "the wounded healer" or "the wounded teacher." He had been shot with a poisoned arrow by his friend Hercules, and was never able to completely heal himself. Yet in his attempts to heal his wound, he ended up saving the life of Prometheus, or Uranus, as astrologers call Prometheus—and in the process of learning how to heal himself, Chiron became a healer to the other centaurs."

I skimmed a few more pages: apparently it's also the place in our Soul that is infused with a sense of aloneness, introversion, and independence. It can be the wound of isolation. Or it can be our healing gift.

I put the book down, and thought about it: So Chiron is about reminding us that there's nothing to fix, cure or get rid of—-sometimes it's simply about accepting what is. That's another word for love, they said. With Chiron we find the key to the wounded healer inside us, and we all have it somewhere in our charts and lives.

How fascinating, I thought. Peter's chart had Chiron in Libra conjuncting Mars. Was he trying to heal some old wound in our relationship that sometimes felt un-healable? Probably. I was wondering how he was doing this.

And so I poured over the charts. My Chiron was in Scorpio in the 7th house of marriage and relationships. Oh yes, I could relate to the pain and holding on to not feeling loved with that aspect. Sophie's was in Taurus in the 11th house of groups and finding one's "tribe." Thomas's Chiron was conjunct his Moon in Cancer and also conjunct Pluto. The book kept repeating that Chiron gives us the choice for forgiveness and deep healing—or bitter resentfulness. Peter's was in indecisive Libra conjuncting Mars. Was it playing out for Peter by some indecisiveness or some ancient inability to move forward?

I looked back at the astrology book and read a little more: "Chiron implies that the inner wound contains a gift. The healing journey of the Soul is the process of discovering the wound as well as the gift. In life, it is the alcoholic that can best cure or "inspire" another alcoholic, because the one who has the wound "knows the territory"....and when our wound is embraced rather than rejected or denied, we can use this new understanding as a key to finding our life direction and soul purpose." Hm...lots to think about there.

What would healing look like for me? I needed to decide so much, and sometimes it seemed as if there was never enough information. Astrology leads to doors of insight, but doesn't say how to go through them. That's our choice.

What would love look like for me now? Was I willing to give Peter another chance even after his having been so "incommunicado" these past months? I didn't know. In Switzerland my heart had opened again to him, but his "waiting" and infrequent emails were more than upsetting—they were almost unforgiveable. Why was there so much back and forth with him?

Just then I heard his feet on the stairs. And then a gentle knock on the door. I jumped up, and we just stood there staring at each other for a second. I detected a quiver in his jaw and his eyes looked glazed.

"Peter! Wow—you're here! "

"I am!" He gave me a big smile and he looked as if he was proud of something. But he simply said "I'm here to help" as he dropped his baggage at his feet. His face had little beads of sweat on it, and I wondered if he felt as if he was poised on the edge of a diving board. But he also radiated something new...was it a fierceness? A sense of courage? Something new...

"Isabelle....I've missed you." Peter looked at me with such tenderness I almost cried on the spot. But I didn't. I motioned him in, poured him a mug of tea, and we sat down...awkwardly.

"I'm sorry. So sorry. Really; about everything that's happened." Peter's voice was the sincerest I had ever heard.

I looked down at the pottery mug I was holding and said nothing. This had been my favorite blue glaze of his on this mug. I let my hands caress the cup.

"Isabelle, I mean it. I'm so sorry...but I couldn't come back until you *asked me* to come back."

I smiled. That's a good start I thought. "I'm sorry too..." I confessed. My finger circled the rim of the cup as if it were circling around all that had been and wondering where to land.

"The fire must have been devastating for you."

I didn't know what to say. I just nodded my head.

Peter stared out the window, and remained silent. Then he reached into his jacket and handed me something. "Before I left Switzerland I was looking for something to bring you—a card or a gift—anything. Then I saw this. I was standing in front of the anniversary cards, and remembered us...how we had been for so many years together. We forgot how good things were, and only remembered the hard times. When I opened this I literally found myself welling up with tears." He handed me the card.

Suddenly, I too was at a loss for words. I felt shy, like a girl getting her first Valentine from the boy she always liked. My hands released their grip on the mug. I took the card and opened it.

"Beautiful, Peter." I could see a photograph on the card's cover of a lake lit up by moonlight. There was a poem inside—I whispered it aloud: *"It doesn't interest me who you know or how you came to be here. I want to know if you will stand in the center of the fire with me and not shrink back. I want to know if you can see beauty, even when it's not pretty….. if you will stand on the edge of the lake with me and shout to the sliver of the moon: Yes!" ~Oriah Mountain Dreamer~*

Inside the card he had written: *I can stand in the fire with you now. I'll love you…always.*

"I can be here for you now in a way I couldn't be here for you before." He paused. "Things got confusing in Switzerland—it's a long story; I'll tell you about it later, but I had to wait till you called, I had to wait until now to come back."

"Okay," I said a bit reluctantly. I could feel scales of anger and hurt beginning to melt away, running like water pouring down from my broken heart…but still, did he have a good reason for making me wait so long? Did he have a reason for not being clear in his emails to me?

"Were you with another woman, Peter?" I asked.

"Only her." He pointed to a guitar case. "I wouldn't do that to you, to us. I was just waiting for the time to be right to come back. I was waiting for you to call me back. You know, you left me, and somehow you had to call me back."

I hadn't ever thought of it exactly that way. About the fact that it was me that left, and me that had to come back to the place in my story where I wanted him again. And I knew I did want him if he was willing to be there with me in "sickness and in health, till death do us part." If he could be in the fire with me...to not leave emotionally. Was he saying he could do that now?

"So what happened?" I demanded. " I need to know why all this waiting?" I pointed to the card. "If this is true, you've got to tell me the truth, now." As I said that, I thought about how the Universe or God was always making us wait. About how Peter made me wait. About how Saturn makes us wait. He makes us wait until the time is right; until we are ready for what is waiting for us. We wait until we can clearly hear the questions—and the answer that emerges. "No transit happens before its time" I thought to myself.

Peter looked down at the floor. His face looked thin...much thinner than I had seen him last. Was he sick?

Peter paused and took a deep breath. "There's good news and not good news. The good news is that when I was over in Zurich...I built this guitar." I looked down at the guitar case next to his suitcase. I wasn't impressed.

"And I found this man who knew how to build these..." He opened the case and stroked the delicate wood of the hand-made guitar.

"So, that was the other woman then! You were building her, while leaving me here! I thought you said you had to be there because you were committed to working at the conference?" I wasn't as happy as he wanted me to be with this good news. "Why didn't you just tell me that? You could have explained."

"I didn't know what to explain. You see, my guitar teacher, this luthier, was like a therapist. I wouldn't admit it even to myself, but I was depressed in a strange way. He noticed it, but I didn't even see it. So I went to this guitar teacher by chance, and as we worked we talked, and he was the man who helped me find words for feelings and to find myself again."

"...and you couldn't have told me about it?"

"No, I was having so much anxiety and couldn't find the words and the feelings inside me. I can imagine now what you were going through back when you left me because I didn't understand about "standing and waiting" to allow the dark times to change and pass. But they do, you know, like moods, and they're not all one person's fault. I just didn't get it then. But I do now."

He rubbed his hands together. "And building the guitar helped me to be patient and regain a piece of myself that I lost. I know it sounds strange, but it's what

I needed to do. And I'm hoping you'll help me keep finding me, as I help you...."

My eyes opened wide. Really...this was it? He went on: "I didn't understand what it must have been like for you to fear that you were going to die, and to have to deal with that by yourself back then. I didn't understand what was happening with me either. Denial and depression can make you do—or not do—lots of things. I think I've been depressed for a long time, since I was a kid, in fact. Sometimes for me to survive I just couldn't allow myself to think or feel too much. I couldn't even allow myself to imagine new possibilities. My guitar teacher said I had "forgotten" a lot. I couldn't be there for you years ago because I couldn't even be present for myself, I just had to work."

I sighed and nodded my head. Peter had Saturn in his birth chart in the fourth house squaring Venus, placed in a way that could point to depression from childhood. His family had taught him to be a good boy and deny his feelings, but I had seen a different part of him starting to emerge in Switzerland. When he brought me to Jung's stone retreat and retrieved the wing of the kingfisher he was daring to do something different. He had been changing all along but I had only glimpsed it.

Then he reached into his pocket. He took out a key and held it in his palm. "This is yours if you want it. It's the key to a place I'll be staying in now...in the North End of Boston. A friend of mine is letting me use his apartment for the next six months while he's away… while I help you rebuild your place…if you want." He held the key in his hand. It looked just like Chiron.

"Is that your plan?" I asked.

"It is, and if you'll say yes, we'll work it out… together." His face looked so hopeful.

I took Peter's key in my hand and stared down at Chiron. Was this the key to his heart—our heart? I could take it; I could choose to re-embrace the history of our common story. The blood rushed to my face.

I took the key and rubbed it like a magic coin, this key that could open more than a door. Here I was the wounded healer at her Saturn Return. The timing of it all felt right; the synchronicity of it all drove my answer out:

"Yes, Peter, yes."

He smiled, and as he did I could see the Peter I always knew and loved. Then he took out his guitar and strummed a few chords…

"The Dutchman's not the kind of man to keep his thumb jammed in the dam that holds his dreams in…but that's a secret only Margaret knows…." He choked up and stopped.

He put down the guitar and reached over to me then—he pulled me so close that for a moment I couldn't breathe. Our eyes were almost touching. I thought how aged and strange we must look to each other at this range. But could we really even see with our eyes at this distance? Could he really see me again now?

"Is that you in there?" he asked, teasingly. He tilted his head so our eyelashes actually came together, the lashes fluttering against each other. We had once called these butterfly kisses.

I remembered this, I remembered how our eyes would squint at the closeness of our faces...could we now learn to be so intimate again and yet not lose our "Self" in our closeness?

"Yes, this is me in here, is that you in there?" I whispered. I felt him in there, behind the hair and wrinkles, behind the eyes and lips, behind the stories and songs. "Yes," he said. "Yes."

The butterfly kiss....and then his lips found mine and he pressed himself against me with such force that it felt as if we had never kissed before—you might say, it drove us over the rainbow. We might say, it was simply us, still here, after all this time. ~

Epilogue

"And to die is different from what anyone supposed and luckier." *Walt Whitman*

December 21, 2040

I know I don't have long to live. I'm curled up on the couch, my aching legs comforted by the antique quilt I'd found the winter my life fell apart. Now, touching the fraying threads, I remember how—long ago—I'd wrap myself in it on those first cold nights after I left my husband of twenty years. Those nightly retreats under the quilt helped me feel connected me to a world larger than myself, an unseen world; a world that was loosely strung together by time and beauty.

I remember stroking the colorful patches and loosely stitched buttons thinking how they'd been sown together by some anonymous woman a hundred years ago—a woman who was perhaps not unlike myself. The comfort of the quilt was one small piece of the tapestry of my life and now it was giving me courage again, just as it had given me courage then.

Tonight however, I'm choosing to be alone for a different reason. I told the visiting nurse not to come, and I told Sophie I'd be going to bed early. I want to be alone with myself in a way I haven't allowed myself to be in a very long time.

All the signs of my upcoming death are approaching. I don't know the exact hour or day, but at my age I can't count on a 'metaphorical' death and re-birth any longer. The physical and astrological signs again feel like a foreshadowing: I'm in my 3rd Saturn Return at 88 years old. Astrologically, it is said that if you live to 84 years it is a full life cycle, as this is the year of the Uranus Return to its birth position. This is often a year of many small epiphanies; and sometimes dying can be one of those...Joseph Campbell and Carl Jung both passed in their 84th year.

I know I've been living on borrowed time and my chances for re-inventing myself are small—except for the ultimate re-invention of dying to this body and opening to the spirit; the ultimate rebirth which I can't control. The astrological indicators feel more predictive than symbolic now, and that's alright with me.

Swat! The wind is slapping that old loose shutter against the window again. Peter would have repaired that if he were alive, as well as all the other things that have gone wrong with the house since he died. I've grown indifferent about keeping up with such things, but I'm not lazy about writing in my journal and talking to the people I love—to those few who are still alive. I still talk to those who have passed over to the other side—and the books, paintings, pottery and kept objects remind me of the fullness of my life. I am grateful.

And there is "Alfie" sleeping and snuggled up in the pillows in the wicker rocking chair, whiskers and tail twitching. He must be having a dream. The clock on the mantel is making its soothing rhythmic sounds—that old clock I made such a fuss about buying, some forty-odd years ago. I've always loved this room, and the way the late afternoon sun streams in through the lace curtains making dancing shadows on the walls. And now I like the way I can see the tiniest sliver of the waning moon from this chair.

I love remembering how Peter and I bought our first house—a little red schoolhouse built in 1794 in Newport. We bought it just before the birth of Sophie. I loved the house passionately the first time I saw it—he said it was overpriced and needed lots of work. I said: "What price can you put on old stone walls and stately maples?"

I pleaded and he sighed. Then he smiled; we bought the old schoolhouse. Peter re-built the wooden frame-work and strengthened the joists; I painted the rooms and gave birth. I remember thinking how the house soon became a safe harbor for us and we felt that we could no more ever leave this house than shed our own skins. But that's what we did—we not only sold the house, but we shed each other like old wineskins before growing the new skins that allowed us to come back together.

And then we bought this 1860's Victorian farmhouse, the house that is the "house of remembering."

It has held us well ever since we came back together again. The walls are permeated by us, as well as by all those who lived here before. Peter used to say I kept too many things here from the past, but this is the way I am. Not a hoarder, but a collector. I treasure objects that have history and meaning—like this house—this house of our "remembering."

❧

Peter's rosewood guitar leans against the wall within easy reach. I pick it up and strum a few chords I remember. Ah...all those minor chords that are still my favorites. If I had to pick my favorite chord, it would be E Minor. What does that say about me? Maybe a little melancholy, but those deep and resonate chords remind me of when Peter and I got back together again.

I love to remember when we met in our twenties—when I was first doing astrology readings and he was making pottery in a shop on the waterfront. I would make a few pots too and help in the shop.

We called our shop 'The Potter's Loft' at first because it had huge windows that looked out over the bay. From its high windows one could see above the gas-lamps and the cobbled-stones of Thames Street. The rent was so cheap back then, partly because the loft was unheated, but we'd turned on the kiln for warmth in the winter and the visitors to Newport always seemed to find this shop. Life was simple enough then so that he could survive on making and selling just a few pots every day. And we had each other.

The ocean is a constant presence in Newport. And the fog horns. I can hear one now—or am I just imagining it? Perhaps I am pretending to remember it now, but back then fog-horns permeated the mists as much as the music and wine did, and we loved the Neptunian atmosphere.

I also loved Peter's luthier art of turning wood into form—and I loved hearing him sing and play. He would often sing poignant love songs; the songs that led me into his heart. His hand-made guitar with its aged varnish seemed to be from an older time; a time that cared more about details and about making things that intertwined and endured. Looking at it now, I see how it has gathered an aura of meaning from years of being handled and played.

And then there was all the pottery. There's not so much left of it now. I want to find a match to light one of the oil lamps that we used to make and sell so many of…instead I pick up a tiny vase and stroke the earthy glaze with my fingers. I can feel the word *Cocroft* etched into the bottom. Pottery and the dream of a family was what had brought us together—we had fallen in love with each other and with hope of a life of possibilities. The jewel of our life together was our daughter, Sophie.

Peter made his first pottery wheel too, like he made his first guitar. And I made and published my two books—writing and books have always been part of my passion.

Who knows what others will remember of us? What will Sophie and her family remember of us? What I remember is that within six months of meeting each other, Peter and I married, and then how twenty years later we separated, and five years after that we renewed our vows. And I remember how "The Potter's Loft" and "Priorities Astrological Counseling" thrived. Astrology was the inspiration and guide that would lead me into this private language of the soul. Astrology was what I was best at, and yet it was always a part of me that few friends understood.

Enough mental ramblings! Where are the matches? I'll need to get up if I want to make this evening special. I want to light the oil lamp again as I have done hundreds of times before. I'm going to enjoy my solitude, make myself a drink, and not explain my actions to anybody.

There's an old saying: "Courage is fear that has said its prayers." I don't know who said it, but interesting how the word courage comes from the French word to "taking heart." I feel as if I need courage. Is remembering a form of praying? Who knows—all I know is that the house feels cold—I must remember to turn the heat up tonight before I go to bed.

I feel a tinge of anxiety. What if I should fall or if someone tries to break in? My neck tenses thinking of these fears and the indignities of old age—I didn't know whether to rage or laugh at the doctor's eyes when he told me yesterday there was nothing wrong with me other than 'old age.' I know what I know, and I know he was wrong.

Squinting in the near darkness, I spot the matches and light the oil lamp. The light is reassuring as I slowly make my way to the kitchen. Reaching down to the lower cabinet I withdraw a bottle of wine. It's open but warm—a little ice will fix that. I open the refrigerator and clumsily pull at an ice tray that refuses to relinquish its hold on the frozen shelf. Damn it! Ah, but there are other ways—and gripping the bottle tightly with both hands, I whack the resistant tray. I don't give up easily; I too am persistent in good ways and bad.

The brittle ice falls in a shower of splinters across the floor, but two cubes lay like gifts in my hand. Opening the bottle I pour myself a large glass.

Making my way back into the living room, I turn on some music and sit again in my chair, the quilt covering my legs. Outside the window I can see the snow beginning to fall. The thick snowflakes will soon cover up the parched brown grass and withered leaves—-I'm glad the remains of summer will not be here tomorrow but will be covered by a blanket of white.

I can see the flickering flame of the oil lamp just beginning to sparkle in the window. The snow is piling up, just like it did that year on the night of the first snow when Sophie was five. She had never been on a sled before and even though it was late in the day I felt there was still a little time left for one quick slide. The Christmas lights gave a glow to the hill and the full moon was going to be coming out soon. It must have been around this time of night. The full moon was just coming up and the snowy crystals were swirling in front of our eyes. But then we went for one last slide down the hill and hit a tree. Sophie cried. Not wanting to break the mood of the night, I licked away her salty tears like a dog, and we howled and romped like two puppies on a chase as we crawled back to our car. I loved her so much.

Oh, this wine is good, even if it's old. It keeps me remembering...all those past lives; the roles of lover, wife, mother, potter, astrologer, divorcee, writer—all those ways I'd dressed and undressed my soul with... until now it feels as if I've become some intricate tapestry of everything I've ever experienced.

'Lightly; lightly...' I whisper to myself. Am I fragile or strong? If only I could get through this last dance of life without any drama. If only the end of my life could be a "falling upwards" with the grace of letting go.

I can see my hand is trembling slightly—is it cold? I take another long sip and a few drops of wine slip down my arm. I love watching the candlelight dance across the deep mirrored surface of the wine. I love the way I feel pulled into the light. Peter used to say I drank too much. I said he didn't drink enough. I poured another glass. It's important to "dream deep" I'd often say. Being Irish always brings out the storyteller in me, and a little wine helps to connect the dots and release the old stories.

And there were always stories; stories that often found their way into the books; books that were like children. A little memoir, a little astrological pondering: part fiction, part non-fiction—I had named and re-named my books like choosing names for children. But no book was as dear to me as Sophie and her family. But the writing? Maybe it was a way to find the threads of meaning that could stitch together the sad and joyful chapters of a life.

I could hear the strains of an old Beatles song as if it came from far away: "Let It be, let it be, let it be, let it be…speaking words of wisdom, let it be, let it be." I let my eyes close. It's cold…the quilt keeps slipping across my lap. I almost fall asleep. No, not yet. I want to remember; I want to go back even farther in time, back to my very first memory; what would that be?

Ah…I can remember peering through the slats in my crib, staring at the peeling paint and spidery cracks on the wall inches from my head. My parents didn't buy me a bed till I was old enough to ask for one. But I remember seeing the wall outside my bed so close up: the rough textured paint made pictures and had a mystery to it; it made me curious about what else was out there in the great world. I wanted to get out of my crib. I wanted a larger life even then.

When I grew a little older I still loved looking at things with different eyes. I remember wondering if there was more to what one saw than what was seen at first glance. I loved peering through layers of crackled oil paint on my grandmother's painting of a "gypsy fortune-teller." I remember that painting in the dining room of my childhood house, and later it took a place of honor in my astrology study. It was dark and textured and hinted of unknown worlds.

Later I would spend many hours staring into another light—the cool light of the computer screen. I would study the luminous mandala-like astrology charts of those who had come to me for readings. I loved the ancient stories of their cryptic markings—the signs, the planets, the angles that spoke to real life events. Those charts gave me a way to inspire people with hope and remind them that "all things will pass". It was a way to talk about what really mattered. It seemed as if a sacred pattern of some other world was hidden there too, a map of our psyche and even past lives might be hidden in the meaning of those circles, squares and stars. I wanted to delve into those mysteries; I wanted to know more, perhaps I wanted to attempt to read the mind of God.

The candle flame is still making new shadows on the wall. I don't feel alone, in fact, there seems to be a multitude of presences here. Breathing in, there's a pull of warmth in the distance; I feel like a moth being lured into the flame. And yet I can relax now and let go of all the stories; I can let go of the wood and clay, the stories. There are low lights moving...the wine glass slides from my fingers. As I move into the dancing shadows I can feel myself being drawn, gladly and freely, through the eye of the needle.

By morning, the snow has covered everything with a blanket of white. I'm still sitting in the rocker with the quilt and a broken wine glass at my feet. Shards of a little vase are on the floor. Sophie has come, and she can see the sunlight bouncing off the wineglass making rainbows on the wall. She will know this is a good sign. She will know I am not very far away.

The house is cold; very cold. The man in uniform keeps explaining to Sophie how it can happen this way to older folks—"hypothermia" he says. She looks shocked. I wish I could comfort her. But I hear him say too, that he's never seen such a peaceful expression on anyone this side of paradise. Sophie smiles when she hears this, but her eyes are watery as she nods and slips the onyx ring off my finger and onto hers. It fits perfectly.

PART TWO

Chapter 1
Saturn and the Saturn Returns

"Know Thyself"

"Nothing in Excess"

What do you think of when you hear the words: *"Know Thyself" and "Nothing in Excess"*? These were the words inscribed above the sacred oracular temple at Delphi, Greece. One might think that by understanding and trying to live by those wise words one might avoid the great troubles in life. Perhaps they help; but still we suffer. The Saturn Returns at ages twenty-nine and fifty-nine are times of great change and opportunity. And so, they can also be times of crisis.

Our understanding of these words changes as we age, but life often plays some nasty tricks on us when we don't get it right. These times require adjustments, and sometimes we don't know what or how to make these adjustments. Perhaps this is why folks who understand "just a little" astrology view the coming of the Saturn Returns with deep sighs. But then, a little knowledge can be a dangerous thing—my hope is that this little book will give you a new look at this old devil, Saturn, to see how you can make "him" work for you.

In writing this, I hope you will experiment with the alchemy that is necessary to take the lead of Saturn and turn it into personal gold. Perhaps you will find this metaphorical gold, and arrive at a deeper understanding of what Oscar Wilde was hinting at when he said: "Falling in love with your Self is the beginning of a lifelong romance."

❧

Saturn is the archetypal symbol of a way of being that slows us down and makes us take a cold hard look at the realities we've built up in our lives. It asks us to change, and it can feel like the voice of the inner critic. In ancient times Saturn was seen as the "old malefic" and its passage was viewed with some suspicion. When Saturn transited across the sky, it spoke of frustration and delay. When astrologers saw Saturn transiting the personal planets in someone's chart, they would counsel seriousness, caution, and careful change. The word itself has roots in the idea of melancholy, timely delay, and the demands of a wise old elder.

However Saturn also represents the arrival of the harvest, and rewards us in the long run for our hard work and effort. It brings a good harvest if we're willing to wait. Its passage in a chart—especially at the times of the Saturn Returns, marks a time when we have an opportunity for deep change and life-renewing rewards.

There are actually three Saturn Returns that happen to everyone if we live long enough: the first is between the ages of twenty-eight and thirty, the second between the ages of fifty-eight and sixty, and the least talked about third transit of Saturn Returning to its birth position, occurs around age eighty-eight. It's necessary to consult the ephemeris or your astrologer to find the exact dates for you, but the feeling of the Saturn Return permeates this whole time period. Astrologically speaking, the first return is when we truly come into our adulthood, the second is when we come into our maturity or elder years, and the third is a reflective time that prepares us to let go of our life when the time is right.

Our culture sees the age of twenty-one as the time of becoming an adult—but not for the astrologically minded. For astrologers it's twenty-nine. And you may get your Social Security at sixty-five, but it's at fifty-nine at the second Saturn Return that your true personal and social security comes up for review. Saturn Returns can be times of rough passage, or harvest, and they're usually a bit of both.

The medieval astrologer, Marsilio Fincino, was the first to express the "gift of Saturn"—namely that the Saturn can be the midwife of insight. This is because depression, or "melancholia" as he called it, creates a permeable boundary between consciousness and unconsciousness, and allows us to adjust issues that have gotten out of hand—real issues—our personal unfinished business. This inner reflection, or depression, is experienced like a "falling into ourselves" that brings us to the point where we are no longer able to continue with life in the usual way. Because we're not nourished any longer by what is—by what the ego has achieved and what the world has given us, we begin creating a bridge: first insight, then action, then change.

So Saturn transits, and the Saturn Returns, are times that can return us to contemplation, peace and equilibrium—or it can lead to what Carl Jung called "enantiodromia"—a complete and opposite change of attitude. This is when a condition is so severe that it polarizes into its opposite. Saturn marks off the stages, the ages, separating time, history and the past. We often lose energy as we move through this passage, as we are called to dance with an invisible partner. The antidote to Saturn is Jupiter, the planet of expansion, grace and opportunities, and Venus, the planet of love and connection and beauty.

During Saturn Returns and transits we may feel that we are in the proverbial: between a rock and a hard place. That no matter which decision we make, it feels as if it isn't the right one. The way isn't clear. It is in these times that we are more permeable to feeling the defeats of the ego and feeling unseen, unloved, and lacking in direction.

Jung would say this space needs to be held and allowed until Saturn brings its gift of insight, creating a bridge for the Self to cross over into a truer destiny path. He talked about this as "holding the tension of the opposites" until the third way (the inspiration or the answer) is made clear. It can arise from the depths of melancholia, but the important thing is to be patient with the process, to wait and to hold the tension within the alchemical vessel of the psyche till the third way percolates up out of the alchemical stew. He counseled waiting, patience, and not breaking the container/vessel by taking the quick and easy way. This is the hard work of Saturn; simply hanging in there until you can see clearly what needs to be done and then gathering your energy to do it.

It seems as if astrologers either want to make light of Saturn transits, or to make them the opposite—fearful. I lean towards seeing the positive restructuring that Saturn wants to build, but I'm aware that it's a mistake to turn the darkness of Cronus (Saturn) into too much of a good thing—for this would miss the fact that what appears to be the dark night of the Soul still is dark (!)—a "Nigredo" experience—even though it's the awakening of imagination. Before movement, there is no movement, or stuckness.

The good news is that although Saturn's passage in our lives marks times of plain hard work and self-questioning, it's also a time when opportunities present themselves to be thoughtfully examined. We need to examine the possibilities and see if we need more time to make changes—to wait—or if we can see clearly what needs to be done, we are called to act and not procrastinate any longer. Like a good cook, you need to know when the soup is done. Undercooking or overcooking will not do. At the times of the Saturn Returns, we are called to be the cooks, the alchemists, and it is the time to claim our authority in our lives whether or not we have done so before.

❧

The first Saturn Return is often marked by personal milestones. We move, marry, divorce, go back to school, have a child, or chose to live differently than we have in our early twenties. The navigational tools are twofold: *you must take a chance now*, and you must give it all you can. If you are willing to do that, you will be rewarded.

Saturn asks us "Whose movie am I in?"" and then challenges us to be the director and author of the movie. Wouldn't it be easier if we could just read some "manual to life" and have the ghost of "Christmas Future" come to us to show the way? Instead, we are called to become our own best "author-ity," to truly become the author of our life.

We're being asked now to re-write our personal life script with our own spiritual muscles. Not always so easy, especially when our life drama is full of people who no longer reflect who we really are and what we are becoming. Letting go of the past is another key concept for this time.

❧

The human unconscious has ways of conjuring up people, events, and situations that challenge us to the bone. Sometimes it seems as if we've conjured up whoever or whatever we most wanted to avoid in our lives. It's as if the unconscious "hires" other people to play out parts of our life stories—this one is the boss, this one the victim, this one the unfaithful lover. At the Saturn Returns you've probably "had it" with some of these people and situations and it's time to write them out of the script of your life drama. At each Saturn Return we are challenged to take back our projections on others and to look at the drama of our life as our responsibility. It's too late to blame anyone anymore.

How does this play out? Perhaps you've held the tension of a bad relationship for a long time, and you've waited and held the tension of the opposites until you've become clear. Then the old lover has finally committed "the last straw" and you know you must end the relationship. You make the difficult break, and a new life begins, with you now being in position to have a real relationship that honors who you are.

Or maybe you've landed a new job, but the learning curve on it sends you home in tears for the first couple of weeks. But you hang in there. You wait and hold the tension of the opposites, and in time, you find you can handle the job and are rewarded with satisfying and challenging work. Or maybe you've wanted to have a child for as long as you can remember, and finally, after much consideration and perhaps much trying, you find you are pregnant. Saturn is often associated with giving birth to something new, but new beginnings, like pregnancies, are not always easy. The gift of the birth though is real and lasts a lifetime.

That's the feeling of the first Saturn Return. If you follow through with a new vision, you've taken the first steps towards a true new beginning. Saturn wants to create new forms and structures and new beginnings, but not without strong foundations. This old father archetype lays the foundational tracks for the imagination train that will follow. This imagination train is in the realm of Neptune, and is the vision we hold while doing the hard work of laying the foundation.

❧

The Second Saturn Return, between the ages of 58-61, is when we grow into becoming a wise elder. It's also a time that calls for concrete actions in the real world, but it's usually easier and more subtle than the first Saturn Return. At this point in our lives, we recognize certain feelings and necessities, and have hopefully found ways to do what needs to be done, and not to be in states of denial.

However, if there have been many times when we've not claimed our own authority, and have lots of unfinished psychic business, it can be subtly insidious. If we don't do what needs to be done now, we might not be given a second chance. If we put off our yearly physical exam or don't stop the spread of some nasty growth, it may be "too late" later. If we take a stiff upper lip attitude and deny the fact that "the job is killing me" it may do just that.

As the body ages, depression and physical difficulties inevitably arise, yet as the body becomes less of an object of strength and vanity it's a new chance for the Spirit to rise. We can find new sources of inspiration for the journey of the "afternoons and evenings" of our lives.

Strangely perhaps, this is also the time when we may feel an uprising of irritability as a few old habits or attitudes have the chance to rear their nasty heads again. This is because now is the time to cut them off—to be done once and for all with them. You may ask yourself: why am I dealing with these same issues again? The answer is: because you've almost resolved them. And the last straw can be the hardest. The hallmark of the second Saturn Return is that if you deal maturely with the old pockets of unfinished business you'll gain the gift that will last till the end—the gift of wisdom.

And how do you do that? It requires a certain amount of humbleness at this age to do this, and not everyone is up to the task. Without enough basic 'ego strength' you may not be able to clean your metaphorical closets and basements of your psyche. It could simply be too painful, or you may need help. This is a time when you are called again to look at your priorities and see if your life is aligned with them or not. There is a need to look at what you feel disillusioned about and to let old illusions go, lest these old ghosts feed on you and make you bitter. It's time to slow down to allow more sweetness, pleasure, usefulness and companionship into your life—a time to let the wild dogs of ambition and fearfulness fight elsewhere.

Yet if we're going to be ambitious, we need to do it in a way in which we can bring the fruits of our life to bear on the project—such as returning to something we already do well, but doing it even better, or perhaps nurturing an old passion or hobby or mentoring someone.

After the passage of the Second Saturn return, when we've cleaned up our own unfinished business, we'll be naturally called upon to pass along what we've learned, especially to the first Saturn Return people who are truly stepping up to the plate now. Sometimes they are our children, sometimes they are strangers or students who we find we can help.

And the third Saturn Return at age 88? Not many people have written about this from personal experience, but the theory is the same. It's a time of deepening understanding, reflecting, and becoming an even Wiser Elder. It would be wonderful if we had "coming of age" ceremonies for each of these transitions, where we could honor these passages and pass down our wisdom to those who are younger.

And lastly, it has often been said that under strong Saturn Returns one can choose between exhaustion and depression—-some choice! It implies that because Saturn is about doing hard work in the real world that exhaustion is the better choice—suggesting as Mark Twain once said: "It is better to wear out than to rust out." If we don't resist it doesn't need to be so tiring. So what are the tools needed to successfully navigate Saturnian waters? Here are a few ideas:

1—*Be Discerning.* You are at a time now when you understand things you didn't understand even last year. Use your new wisdom to make wise choices based on clarity of intention. Dream into your future and discern the path through the woods. Here is where the quotes: "Know thyself" and "Nothing in Excess" become relevant. At these times there is a necessity to pull back from the excesses of your younger years and to know what you can and cannot do.

2—*Take Heart.* Find ways to reach out to others and be humble enough to ask for advice. If your marriage is in trouble, ask yourself the question: Is the relationship the true source of dissatisfaction, or is it the repository of your own misery? How much are you projecting your insecurities onto your partner, and not taking responsibility or even listening 'with heart'?

3—*Go Deeper.* Superficial "all or nothing" solutions can be a quick fix and Saturn doesn't like quick fixes. No quick decisions: instead, hold the tension of the opposites and conflicts within yourself till you see the emergence of a new idea. Then, and only then, is it time to stretch beyond your comfort zones to new places of thought and action. As was said so many years ago, by Marcus Antoninis: "Dig deep; the water—goodness—is down there. And as long as you keep digging it will keep bubbling up."

4—take *Action.* Saturn ultimately rewards those who act and depresses those who procrastinate indefinitely. In ancient texts, Saturn was sometimes seen as a devil who made a hand signal that said: "All that you see, is all there is." That's the devil's lie, and it saps motivation. You can prove him wrong by changing your life.

So Saturn can be seen as the spirit of Father Time, passing through our lives at these transits and "Returns" in the way Scrooge experienced his encounter with the Spirits of the past, present, and future. The purpose of these visits wasn't to give Scrooge a bad case of nerves, but to give him a second chance at life. He saw himself differently; he grieved, he tried denying and avoiding, but ultimately he *acted*, and propelled himself—just in time—toward his new life.

So blessings on your Saturn Returns! These times of initiation give you a unique window of opportunity to finish what you've come into this life to do. It won't be perfect, but now you'll have a little more insight into what this transition is about and how you might work with it gracefully. Thoreau summed it up well when he said: "We are constantly invited to be who we really are." The writer George Eliot takes it a step further:" It is never too late to be what you might have been." Now is the time to *go for it*...measure twice, cut once.

When we make the little things in life sacred, we honor life. When we think of the astrological planets as ancient gods, then we "honor the gods" when we give them what they ask of us. We know that the ancients once believed this: that when we give *the gods* what they want, they would *give us* what we want. So we can take this as an experiment, and honor our rationality as well as our often fearful minds. Saturn does ask for something in particular from each one of us, and in these pages you will see how using the *descriptive sign and house placement* of your Saturn will help you discover your true Self.

So take a look at your chart first. If you don't have your chart, go to the internet and google "free astrology chart" and you will enter your birthday and year and place to get your chart. One of the most popular sites for this is www.astro.com but there are others. Then, find where your Saturn is in your birthchart: it looks like the letter "h" done in calligraphy! Next to it will be a number (not important for this) and a glyph that is the *sign* your Saturn is in—it will be in one of the 12 signs from Aries to Pisces. Then look to see what section of the chart it is in—that's called the "house." Your chart may have the house numbers on them, or if not, it's the same for everyone: it works like *a clock* with "house one" starting at nine o'clock and going to eight o'clock, and "house two" starting at 8:00 o'clock and going to 7:00 o'clock…the houses always going backwards in number around the clock to "house twelve" which would be the section of a clock between 10:00 and 9:00 o'clock.

Now you know the sign and house of your Saturn. Read about it twice in the following pages, first for the sign, and then again for the house. The sign and house are different but similar—astrology is not an exact science! *The sign* is like an adjective, describing the nature of your Saturn, and the house adds more description to that. *The house* also suggests what area of your life Saturn is playing out in. So read your Saturn placement by sign and house, and then use your intuitive psyche to combine the two to hear what is being asked of you. And remember, that a "Saturn Return" at 29, 59, and 88 are times when Saturn has circled, or transited the whole chart, and returned to its home position after roughly 29 years of moving through each house in a counter-clockwise position.

Chapter 2

Saturn in Aries, or Saturn in the 1st House

The sign of Aries is about finding your courage, acting on it, and accepting your limitations. You need to make the effort to take risks, and to actively engage with life through speaking up and physically testing yourself, despite fears of rejection or failure. You may have developed a persona or mask in which you fool yourself into thinking you are already very brave—but astrologically speaking—you are being *called to* bring out those qualities. Stress and challenge bring out qualities of courage when you say "yes" to opportunities as they arise.

Choose your battles wisely with Saturn in Aries. You are often good at starting things, but may struggle to complete the task. At times you may feel yourself to be a loner with the "loneliness of the long distance runner." It's a mood you may be familiar with....but hang in there. Choose the challenge, and stay with it.

With Saturn in this position you tend to have a provocative blend of being intensely confrontational one moment, and reluctant to "showing yourself" the next moment. You may not even know how much innate charisma and energy you have, although others can feel it and love you for it—still you are probably the only one who knows how much you've had to "feel the fear and do it anyway."

When you choose to blaze a new trail and risk daring to be all you can be, you do well as long as you are willing to honor your limitations and those of others…not always easy for you! Sometimes it's easier to "butt heads" Aries style with whoever appears to be the boss or authority in any given situation—but this is a defensive reaction. You don't need to do that.

Instead at your Saturn Returns you can explore which boundaries you will choose to honor, and which you choose to challenge. You can still be impulsive at times, but you're learning how to be savvy and smart enough not to sabotage yourself while testing your limitations. You know there are great heights you can explore and you've fallen in a few valleys. When you were young, you probably learned the hard way what kind of behavior was acceptable or not, and now at each Saturn Return you get a chance to courageously step into your next adventure. Go for it!

Saturn Return Question: There's an old saying that those who obey all the rules miss most of the fun. Who knows how much of that is true—but—with Saturn in Aries you could fall victim to that. Dare to experiment so that you know what works for you and what doesn't. When do you sabotage yourself by being too confrontational or too reserved? Is there a better balance you can achieve? How can you speak and act on your truth more skillfully? You might even want to dare yourself to "hang in there" with projects until they are done to your satisfaction—don't give up too easily, especially when you're close to the finish line!

Chapter 3
Saturn in Taurus or Saturn in the Second House

With Saturn in Taurus there can often be a "fear of loss" both subtly and not so subtly. Saturn's lesson in Taurus is to teach the individual how to develop his self-worth by discovering and upholding his true sense of values and priorities, independent of society's judgment. There are several challenging manifestations with this placement.

Saturn in Taurus appreciates the fine things in life, but still may be coming from a sense of scarcity psychologically. There's a desire for the good things in life and stability—emotional, financial, and spiritual. Taurus would like clear uncomplicated answers. But life is paradoxical and often messy, so this in itself upsets those who have Saturn placed in Taurus.

Taurus has an affinity (or 'issues' as we often say!) with food, beauty and money—so Saturn here tests our relationship with each of these things. Physically, it effects how we feel about our body; the manner we perceive ourselves physically, and how susceptible we are to social pressures about our looks. If other planetary parts of our charts are rebellious and are non-conforming there can be even more challenges, as Saturn in Taurus can manifest as a love-hate struggle with food, money, diet, exercise, and the process of aging.

Similar to other earth signs, Saturn in Taurus can be a workaholic who can experience guilt and shame for indulging in the rewards of hard work. In a sense you could see yourself as "being tested" for knowing and living by your true sense of values. If possible, don't make material things too important or try to possess loved ones. Let them love you for just who you are.

Saturn in Taurus is persistent to the point of stubbornness, and has great stamina and loyalty. You can be very pragmatic, restricting yourself in the present, and with careful planning you may put off immediate gratification for the promise of future reward, and it will often pay off!

If Saturn is afflicted by difficult aspects, money isn't denied, but there may be problems in under or over spending—the same goes for the use of your sexual energy. Find the balance between too much and too little. The 2nd and 5th chakras are involved here, so sexual as well as throat and speech issues can be important. But because something is "challenging" doesn't mean it's bad or lacking, in fact, when you meet the challenge, you may very well find you have gifts in precisely those areas in which you are challenged!

Many people with Saturn in Taurus or the second house, have created a skill for dealing with finances, for healing themselves through nature and music, and have "tweaked" their values and priorities just enough so that they don't have to bolster their self esteem with over-indulgences or spending. You already have, and own, what you need. When you really know that, you'll be happier and wiser.

Saturn here motivates one to discipline, structure, and 'grounding'. Saturn here, or in the third house, will teach lessons of trust, patience and self-worth. Many people with this placement achieve what they want in life because they are willing to bring their loyalty and persistence to long-term plans and goals. "Slow and easy wins the race" was written for this placement of Saturn.

Saturn Return Questions: When do I sabotage myself by being too slow to respond or too fearful to take a risk? Could I give myself more time to ponder what my true beliefs are, and act from them, rather than "reacting" to outside pressure or expectations? Do I cultivate—and let myself appreciate—the joys of loyal friendships? What would happen if I changed my mind about some old assumptions?

Chapter 4

Saturn in Gemini, or Saturn in 3rd House

With Saturn in Gemini you are challenged to explore everything that excites your curiosity and to express it! Talk, write, sing, teach, share what you've experienced—be a bridge builder for those of us who don't "know" what you know. You are meant to be a communicator, but ironically you may be underestimating yourself because learning and speaking as a child may not have come easily for you. You may have stuttered, felt shy, or not felt up to the challenges you saw around you in school—or perhaps because you were simply bored. If you felt overwhelmed with details you may have skipped out on learning certain things, because what you wanted was to uncover the more interesting facts and the emotional truths of situations. That's not always what they teach in schools.

Saturn in Gemini is about the mind, and using it—so take what you know and go deeper—put your spin on it. Whether you sing it out, paint it, or write it out, you have the flexibility and willingness to explore all sides of a story. You can handle chaos and you're wise when you bring all the details together to make thoughtful decisions—joining your intellect with the values of your wisest self. You are meant to become a "magician" with your mind. You can teach us or fool us, you can be a teller of white lies or a con artist, or you can gather up all the "news" and astound us with the connections and insights. You can bring new understandings to the rest of us, showing that life is more complex and magical than we thought.

When Saturn transits a sign, that's where you must "get it together" in the qualities of that sign. It's as if a spotlight is shining on wherever Saturn is transiting. So here, in this position, you are called to be expansive and to communicate *skillfully.* Learn how to raise communication to a new art. At your Saturn Returns, you may have unfinished business with your siblings, your car, short journeys, and self-esteem. Find little ways to pay attention to the minor and often annoying details in life so that they don't trip you up. Get the oil changed on the car, decide to always put your keys in one place, and—yes—take your vitamins. Little things count a lot with Saturn in Gemini. Health wise, it rules the lungs, and smoking would be particularly unwise for you. So ask yourself, what still needs to be dealt with in my life that I've been denying or distracting myself from doing? The time of the Saturn Return calls you to take action, deliberately and consciously to heal and finish whatever "business" still is unattended to in those areas.

Saturn Return Questions: When Saturn has come around again to its birth place in your chart, it's a good time to take stock of your life. Have you let too many distractions and diversions pulled you away from what you really love? Don't let Mercury, the ruler of Gemini, sabotage your long range goals…it's never too late to be who you might have been…and if you're feeling overworked, consider what Mark Twain once said: "I'd rather wear out than rust out."

Chapter 5

Saturn in Cancer or Saturn in the Fourth House

Saturn helps us come into our personal authority and authenticity by demanding that we create structures in our lives that have integrity. Here we see an emphasis on creating an emotional and physical foundation for "home, heart and hearth." It is also a summons to look at how you've chosen to tell the story of your life—are you the hero or victim? Could the story be reframed more accurately? The 4th house and Cancer have a lot to do with the "mythology" of our lives. What is the emotional truth and what is the factual truth? When does it matter if there's a difference?

Saturn helps us to define our limitations and boundaries as well as those of others. Saturn is often associated with the father, the paternal, and all that is authoritarian. So when placed in the more maternal feminine sign of Cancer or in the fourth house, it is said to be in its "detriment" because the paternal and maternal often challenge each other, until consciousness is brought to the family karmic inheritance. Old adjectives such as 'detriment' are not so useful anymore because the gifts of Saturn in Cancer are great, and these old terms need to be seen with fresh eyes.

However it might be wise to ask yourself if you are carrying old pains, restrictions, melancholy, or guilt about your family of origin with Saturn in Cancer. You can choose to reflect upon and heal some of those old issues with a therapist and reframe the personal mythology of your life. You can make it a priority to make your home situation the most ideal that you can imagine. Your home is important to you—you tend to act protectively in relation to your home and family, which is a good thing. Yet you can get so enmeshed in control issues around family problems, so the challenge for you is to truly understand what you feel and not to be reactive to things from the past.

Often people with this placement feel an emotional allegiance to the place where they grew up, and yet have an awareness that in many ways they have had a strict or difficult upbringing—or there may have been a mood of emotional coolness underlying something in the family dynamic. Secrets may have been kept, or there may have been rules as to what children could and could not do—rules or assumptions that may have caused some suffering.

Because you are now willing to work hard at making your own family a success you will often go out of your way to try and not repeat the problems of your own childhood by working extra hard to guide and care for your own children. You may become gifted in solving family problems because you know the territory.

With this placement of your Saturn, you have the opportunity to come into a more balanced inner sense of authority—I think of this as becoming the "author" of your own life script—and to create and restore a bit of sanity between the archetypal influences of the feminine/maternal with the masculine/paternal.

Saturn Return Questions: Have you been able to understand and share with someone else the deep resonance and sometimes confusing feelings you grew up with? Do you know how your family of origin has influenced you? Have you answered the inner call to settle old hurts with your parents or siblings and change past patterns of relating?

Chapter 6

Saturn in Leo or Saturn in the Fifth House

Saturn in Leo or in the fifth house, hungers for love. But no one else's love will ever fulfill that hunger except your own love and self-respect. Oscar Wilde once wrote: "Falling in love with oneself is the beginning of a life-long romance." And if you think of that quote as speaking not of narcissistic self-love, but of loving your higher true Self, then there is a deep level of truth spoken here. And this is something you don't have to depend on other people to give you.

It's important for people with Saturn in Leo or the fifth house to find the courage within them selves to dare to express themselves openly with heart and passion! Leo rules the physical and emotional heart, and generosity of spirit is crucial to this sign. Saturn however, tends to put a damper of frustration, delay, or inhibition on whatever sign it's in until we've committed ourselves to our "work" and here the work is in loving yourself. Even Jesus said that it was important to: "Love your neighbor as you love yourself." Sometimes we think of the feelings towards the neighbor and forget that self-love and respect comes first.

Saturn here calls us to become a disciple to our Self—that is, when we realize that "disciple and discipline" are related, we become a disciple to our Self. We can become committed to the highest expression of ourselves. And it can be fun—not self-centered! Leo is called upon to "shine" and express what we all have in our hearts and minds.

If you have Saturn in Leo or in the fifth house, it might be wise to create an intention around your creativity. You have a charismatic emotional impact when you choose to use it, and because you are aware of how risky and dramatic your life can be, you have the potential gift of expressing this drama artistically or playfully in your life. Don't feel guilty about being fun-loving or playful. It is by "following your bliss" as Joseph Campbell once said, that you find the best way for your talents to come forth. If you find that you don't have enough time or opportunity for "fun," then schedule it in! Don't hold yourself back in an effort to be too modest, or to engage in solitary discipline that never finds expression in the world. Working hard is great, but remember to allow yourself to joyfully express who you really are.

Saturn Return Questions: How can I give myself permission to dare to do things my own way? Could I make an effort to spend more time with my paints, my music, my writing, or my loved ones? Am I working too hard and becoming "up-tight"? Where and when can I dare my Spirit to truly find release? "Now" might be a good answer to that question.

Chapter 7

Saturn in Virgo, or Saturn in 6th House

Priorities and details—these are the key words for Saturn in Virgo and the 6th house. Oh my goodness, that doesn't sound like much fun, does it? But with this placement you will actually have more joy and a richer life if you keep circling back to prioritizing things, including bringing awareness to how you spend your time each day, to staying healthy, and cultivating an attitude of "awareness" to the details of the moment. It can be as simple as "being completely here and now." Saturn here also suggests that besides the daily attention we must bring to our work, and our health, we are asked to "teach and be taught." Mentoring and apprenticeship are keywords for Virgo and the sixth house.

If you think of creating priorities and paying attention to details as "shoulds" you may rebel against them, or you can re-frame it. This is what the philosopher Krishnamurti did when he repeatedly asked us to "wake up" and bring our full awareness into what we are doing with ourselves in the moment and in the course of our lives. In even simple things such as "uncluttering" your world from too many distractions, your self-expression and creativity and joy has more room to come forth.

With this placement you are often blessed with a certain wisdom of the larger scope and questions of life, and you seem to hold a wisdom that the rest of us don't have—you hold a unique knowing of the Ideal that is special to this astrological position. But it will be important to your personal success to bring awareness to the "little things in life" by bringing skillful attention to the flow of events in your daily life. Learning how to discriminate between what is important to do at the moment, and what is superfluous will be critical. Your heart is in the right place; it's getting your head down to this reality that's sometimes the challenge.

Another challenge—and opportunity—for you is to learn the most skillful means of doing things. Taking the time to master techniques and tools, whether it is life skills such as cooking and caring for your child, or mastering a trade or profession—these are important. If you can be humble enough to allow yourself to be mentored and to learn from others, the process will be easier and more efficient. You don't always have to re-invent the wheel! Until Saturn in Virgo or the 6th is mastered, you may suffer from misplacing your talents, from dis-ease, and the continual sense that things are breaking down or getting lost—i.e. "mercury is retrograde" could feel like a life-long disease.

Saturn Return Questions: How can I prioritize what is really important to me? How can I make definite moves and a strategy to bring this about? How can I pay better attention to the details of my life and my time management so that I succeed in what I truly care about? And while doing this, can I manage to take better care of my health on a daily basis?

Chapter 8
Saturn In Libra or Saturn in the Seventh House

Here we have the alchemy of relationships on the front burner. With Saturn in Libra or in the seventh house we are "cooking" with the temperature on high! In order not to burn away the *goodness* we are required to balance the ingredients and hold the opposites in a delicate way. Compromise, negotiation, respect, and fairness must enter the mix. Of course you think you know that—but are you ready to have the love and relationships now you feel you deserve? Will you dare? What happens when you get it—or almost get it? Can you receive the love? Are you ready to do the dance of giving and receiving?

It's not as simple as it sounded years ago. It takes both humility and personal strength to engage in this dance, and Saturn tends to cast a dark eye on impractical or overly-romanticized relationships. Power struggles and emotional grid-lock arise before we know how to do this dance well. There will be limitations or blockages in relationships until we have learned to go beyond *the urge to control* for "personal" reasons. Some call this sweet manipulation.

Who me, you might say? Don't we know all about co-dependence and inter-dependence? Yet with this aspect we are more keenly aware than ever that we can only go so far by ourselves. We thought we had this figured out a long time ago when co-dependence was the nasty word of choice—when we thought we could see clearly who needed to take on more personal responsibility, and when we shifted from *victim to hero* on our soul's journey. Or did we?

Now, Saturn is passing through Libra for all of us in 2011 and 2012 and so we are being required to understand this on a new level. Saturn always creates tests and challenges in whatever sign it is passing through, and if you have this aspect in your birth chart you'll be "cooking" even more in the relationship arena.

Saturn is said to be exalted in Libra for many reasons, but as an air-mental sign Libra is willing to do the work involved in finding new ways of thinking that create "win-win" situations. Again, familiar words, but can you stop seeking approval from *everyone* and maintain a strong sense of self as you merge with others? When disagreements arise in relationships, what are you going to do about the inequalities of feeling that become evident? Can you tolerate listening to someone speak their "Truth" when it's so radically different from the Truth you hold dear?

It's a challenge to know when to turn the temperature *down* to a comfortable acceptance of differences, and when to stand in your Truth on *high heat and say this is not acceptable?* Not easy when you're feeling pushed towards a reality that is more than you've been comfortable with so far. That's Saturn in Libra. Saturn in the seventh house means your Saturn is playing out in the relationship arena of marriage and close partnerships.

Saturn Return Questions: Take a look at the social contracts, expectations and assumptions you hold with significant others, now and in the past. Was it clear to them what you expected and hoped for? Was it realistic to ask them for this, or did you expect them to "mind read"? If you feel as if you've been giving (or gave) too much or you're feeling abandoned, you might be able to prevent it happening in the future by being a better communicator. Or you might realistically understand that you were asking too much of someone—you might have been asking someone to do something they were not able to do at the time. Most of us do the best we can with what we know at the time. It's not always enough.

Now, as you are being called to be the best you can be, you are being called on to be incredibly honest as well as tactful. This is not "the Libra" that is always pretty and poised and fair, it's about radical understanding of yourself and others. Are you willing to engage in this dance?

Chapter 9

Saturn in Scorpio, or Saturn in the Eighth House

Saturn in Scorpio or in the Eighth house, by birth or transit, brings up issues around money, sex, inheritance, and attempting to control others. Wherever Saturn is in the chart, is where there are subtle and deep psychological patterns that reflect challenges to be overcome. As we meet these challenges, the fear that motivates Saturn to fight, flee, or try to control all begin to lose their grip on us.

A Pluto ruled Saturn is associated with that which is occult or hidden, even within yourself. Take time to look at your own inner judgments that may be oppressing you, and draw them out to explore them. Find ways to release them. It is here that the "unknown" can arise in your life and you find that through sex, or sharing resources with others—especially money—you are fearful of being controlled, or fearing loss. You may find yourself in a burden of debt, or fearing that others won't be there to support you emotionally or financially.

Buying a house together or investing money with another person or even having to deal with banks, can bring up fears you may not have been aware of before.

What's happening here? In many ways you're hoping to find correct 'boundaries' between yourself and others, but the fear of abandonment, entrapment, debt, and losing emotional control can be frightful. With Pluto ruling Scorpio and the Eighth house, one could say that the best attitude here is one of surrender and a 'discerning acceptance' but this is never easy.

Saturn feels the expectations of others, wants to be responsible, and yet is quite uncomfortable not feeling secure in knowing how much to give and how much to hold back. Fairness and equality are sought after, but emotional power struggles can still arise from the depths. Messy divorces with financial complications can be an expression of this, and yet the real issue is not money but self-respect, personal power and independence. We may need to learn how to be independent from others without sacrificing our Souls. We need to understand that our bank accounts, our shared resources, and even our fears of emotional intimacy are being acted out here, and that love of Self and Other are more closely entwined than we ever guessed.

Saturn Return Questions: So what to do in the face of this fear? "Love God, and tie your camel" isn't a bad response. Pluto has also been known as the "God of Wealth" but true wealth is not winning a messy court battle, but being savvy, playing fair, and going deeper...

looking at the roots of whatever poverty you may be feeling. It can be good to remember that you have within yourself and within your relationships a wealth that can be truly humble and fair. That generosity of spirit gives a person true wealth.

With Saturn here, either in the birth chart or by transit, or in the Saturn Returns, we might be wise to learn the difference between loneliness and solitude. In solitude we gain confidence in ourselves, nurture our Souls and creativity, and learn that we don't need to conform to the other people's expectations. We can create proper boundaries, and know when to give and take. We pay our taxes, balance our checkbooks, and remember the depths of our resources. We are greater than the sum of our parts and generosity feeds our hearts more than any money or power could ever do.

Chapter 10
Saturn in Sagittarius, Saturn in the Ninth House

Here we have the call of the spiritual journey—the "work" of Saturn in Sagittarius or the 9th house is about learning what brings meaning to life. Sounds easy? Not quite….this is not the typical religious journey, with its call to hand over spiritual authority to someone else, but the call to seek personal meaningfulness in this life. This quest for knowledge and understanding is like the rudder of a boat for you, very necessary for you to maintain your equilibrium.

With Saturn here, it's not about accepting traditional religion with the image of a god who is all knowing and all judging—in fact, with this placement, you're likely to find some ideas in the Old Testament or any patriarchal system to be quite distasteful! (Yes, this could translate into any situation at home or at work where you feel as if you don't have any authority to experiment and feel free to find your own way.)

But...you'd like "to be right" and even be a bit of the arm chair philosopher at times. You have a hunger for wisdom and a delight in telling a story. You may be persistent, humorous and have a tolerant view of life, yet at your core there's a hunger for something more. You want to get your relationship with God and Life right—even if you're an atheist. You want daily work that has meaning, and a life you can be proud of. Who doesn't? But your ability to set priorities and "focus in" can make the rest of us look spiritually lazy...for you are on the right path when you make the effort to travel, study and come into right relationship with your Self.

Some astrologers might see this Saturn placement as being one of the "reluctant philosopher." It sounds easy, but the search for wisdom often leads us on paths that travel right through hell before we get it right. You don't get this hunger for Truth, fairness, and spiritual equality by being in a state of bliss—it's more likely you've seen and lived through the worst, and passed through the shadows of prejudice, constriction, and narrow minded injustice. Most of us are reluctant travelers through the realms of hell.

Saturn Return Questions: With Saturn, the planet of "concentrated focus" in expansive Sagittarius, you will be challenged to see both sides of any issue and to hold the "tension of the opposites" in your life until the gleam of understanding and wisdom breaks through. Don't give up! As you willingly hold two opposing viewpoints or have to choose between "a rock and a hard place" make a decision to wait and ponder before acting. The right answer will arise in time. Can you set your own self-generated priorities and find what brings inner freedom for you? You are being called to be a wise person who will teach the rest of us the true meaning of freedom, tolerance and love. But no short cuts are allowed—you can't do a spiritual bypass on emotional problems. One step at a time...and you're there. Not so bad!

Chapter 11

Saturn in Capricorn, or Saturn in the 10th House

With Saturn in its own natural sign and house, there can be a strong desire to be recognized for who you really are, and the good work that you do—for you are one who can handle burdens, take on responsibility, be in charge, and do the job well. Are you getting credit for it? This theme of responsibility and shouldering burdens can echo back to a desire to be recognized and respected by a parent—when you were young, did you have your 'injustice' heard and were you seen for who you really were? Nothing is perfect, but for you there may still be the desire to get back from the world what you didn't get from a significant parent or mentor.

Although you are quite willing to work hard and cautiously, sometimes you can be hindered by too much cautious behavior or fear of disapproval...so sometimes you may try to control situations and obey the rules too tightly, and then find yourself revolting against your own behavior! This can be a way to self-sabotage so it's important for people with Saturn in Capricorn or the 10th house to give themselves credit and self-approval, and not to dismiss their own efforts. You are often better than you realize.

"Who am I in the eyes of the world?" is an important question for you, yet the danger is about becoming too identified with what you do and stuck in your own ways. Who are you trying to please? What limits and boundaries are truly right for you—it's important for you to judge what is fair and right for you and your beliefs, and not just for other's expectations or approval.

Saturn in this position shouldn't be difficult, but it often is. You may be holding standards of excellence that make it almost impossible for you to live up to. You can be hard on yourself. In fact, you may have taken on burdens of caregiving or doing what "is right" and then find yourself at one of your Saturn Returns saying: "Now what am I going to do when I grow up?" If this is you, don't despair, as Saturn "ripens as it ages" and deep fulfillment often comes later in life. You know how to depend on your own resources, you are a good organizer, and now you can allow yourself the chance to dream into new and different possibilities.

Saturn Return Questions: Am I still inwardly trying to gain approval from someone other than myself? How do I really "feel" about things? Saturn here can make it easy to think about things, but not so easy or clear to know how we really feel about things. If love or approval wasn't given to you early in life, you can still gain that love and respect through attainment of your ambitions and you can gain the love you want by giving it. When you give a "good think" about where you are in your life, make sure that you are playing by your own rules and sense of integrity. That is what is truly important, and will lead you where you want to be. And in all of this, continue to be good to yourself, and to soften that inner critic—you deserve it! You are more loved and respected than you know.

Chapter 12
Saturn in Aquarius, or Saturn in the Eleventh House

With Saturn in Aquarius or in the Eleventh house your "work" is around groups and the world of ideas. Books and rich conversations feed your Soul. You are karmically connected to the ideals of your "tribe"—your friends and any group focused around some common purpose. For good or bad, this "non-blood-related" family is important for you.

And yet it is common to find a strong feeling of social isolation with those who have Saturn in Aquarius as there is a keen sensitivity to the "shoulds and oughts" of your culture, and the social and political groups you find yourself in. Just as you might feel yourself to be an outsider in your family of origin in some way, you might also feel an outsider in groups even if you have a strong presence in them. The past, particularly within your family, is reworked in the present among these new pcoplc, and you are called to find a way now that you can be comfortable fitting in with your "tribe" or friends or community.

With Saturn in the 11th house of Aquarius you are challenged to know about what your unique personal ideals are, what you believe in, and how you can find kindred spirits in the world. Of course, nothing is a perfect fit, but still you try, as you know you need to interact with others so as to stabilize your purpose in life and to overcome fear of disapproval.

Do you know what you think, what you believe in, what you consider worthy or fun, and what matters most to you? Have you thought about how you have been conditioned by your family and the culture to conform? This re-assessing can be a continual and changing "problem." Saturn here is called to be flexible (not natural to 'him'!) and to change as your ideas and ideals change, and as your friends and alliances change. If this isn't done, there can be a revolt in your psyche, and a tendency to be eccentric, extreme, or socially insecure if you haven't given yourself the inner time to know what you stand for, and who you stand with. It doesn't matter what others think of you, but it does matter what you think of yourself and the attitude you project to others.

Aquarius and the 11th house is future oriented, and so goals, intentions and strategies carry a lot of importance for you. You are being challenged to become the person you truly are—not any imitation of yourself. Carl Jung referred to this as the call to "individuation." People with Saturn or many planets in Aquarius or the 11th house often come into "their unique sense of themselves" later in life as they've worked out issues around duty, rights and freedom. They can stand alone or with others, and they can just as easily be the loners among groups as they can be the leaders of groups. And in time, these positions can change.

Saturn Return Questions: What really makes me happy? What really makes me sad? What do I hear about on the news that I "can't stand?" Is there any way I can find a way to be in the world where what I love to do or what I care about most, could be my "work"? Where can my gladness meet the world's needs? How can I turn my anger at injustice and stupidity into something helpful? Aquarius relates to revolution and evolution, but first you truly need to know just where you stand. Think about it…

Chapter 13

Saturn in Pisces, Saturn in the 12th House

There is a "great longing" for union and transcendence of the mundane with Saturn in Pisces or the 12th house. It is a place where the invisible activity of the deep psyche is stirred. This is the area of the personal and collective unconscious; the "house that Carl Jung built." It is also the place where subtle unfelt feelings, unfinished business and illusions live, and with this placement there can be a fear of emotional "drowning or dissolving" if too much time and energy is spent with the burdens of everyday life. Time needs to be given to the deeper supports and structures that uphold you, and where you can discern the difference between illusions and imaginative possibilities. How do you reconcile dreams and the demands of reality? Here is where the needs of your psyche must be tended to with a loving and accepting attitude.

As the first paragraph implies, this is not an easy thing to do, although one would think it would be as easy as sitting outside on a summer's day contemplating clouds. Often one cannot do this for longer than five minutes. There is a longing for imagination here and a yearning for meaningfulness that can be expressed positively through contemplative arts such as music, painting, or writing, or through compassionate activities that don't rely solely on left brain rational thinking.

With Saturn in Pisces or in the 12th house you are called to give yourself a break—you may find yourself moving away from structures that no longer serve you. This letting go can generate that fear of dissolving or drowning, but what is really happening is that the old ways are being washed away so that a rebirth of something better can take place.

There's a need with this placement to express one's sensitivity and emotions and yet to make one's higher vision and yearnings practical and real. Discipline and routine can be helpful when it keeps distractions away and gives one the space to creatively and personally get to know oneself. Often there's a desire to escape from reality in some way—addictions can spring from anxiety and attempts to control too much by rigid habits or ways of thinking that can thwart the higher expression of Saturn in Pisces in the 12th house.

Saturn Return Questions: Do you feel uncomfortable in some groups? Are you feeling a need to withdraw from time to time? Why not allow yourself to turn "alone time" to creative solitude, and allow yourself to feel comfortable with the more subtle impressions that you may be feeling? Can you talk about this with a friend and find ways to express the hidden gold that you are mining? You are flowing into new territory and you'd be wise not to defend yourself behind tight boundaries. The water wants to flow within you, and simply be contained by gentle boundaries.

For Those Who Are Curious~

If you are interested in learning more about astrology or about having a personal reading of your chart, take a look at the bottom of the homepage at: www.elizabethspring.com for details. I can also be contacted at: elizabethspring@aol.com

My first book, "North Node Astrology; Rediscovering Your Life Direction and Soul Purpose" is also available through amazon.com—this book is particularly useful for understanding the changing nature of transits in your life, and the important significance of the North and South Nodes. Explanations of the Nodes by sign and house are there, along with a chart that enables you to find these Nodes based simply on your birth day and year.

Elizabeth Spring, M.A. has a degree in psychology with an emphasis in the work of Carl Jung. She is an astrologer, psychotherapist, writer, and occasional teacher. Her work in astrology is influenced by archetypal psychology as well as evolutionary astrology, and she has been certified by Steven Forrest, an evolutionary astrologer, and endorsed by James Hollis, Jungian analyst and writer. Elizabeth lives in Wickford, Rhode Island, with her husband, a potter and musician, and her daughter, son-in-law, and two grand-daughters.

"Saturn Returns; The Private Papers of a Reluctant Astrologer" is fiction, although the non-fiction information on Saturn and the Saturn Returns is accurate and meant to be used for "all who are curious" about their lives and the language of astrology.

Printed in Great
Britain
by Amazon

31554239R00177